He was standing

Turning from him, she... space between them... stupid that she would... put a little distance between them, she was going to wind up making love with him.

And that would add a whole new set of complications to an already tenuous situation, she thought ruefully.

She suddenly became aware of the fact that the silence between them was intensifying. It made her even more uneasy.

"Um, maybe I should make you dinner," Bailey said.

Walking away from Wyatt, she had every intention of going to the kitchen and doing just that.

But Wyatt caught hold of her wrist, stopping her. When she looked quizzically at him over her shoulder, he slowly turned her around.

"Is that what you really want to do?" he rasped.

His dark blue eyes were holding her prisoner. Bailey found that she could barely draw in a breath.

* * *

**The Coltons of Roaring Springs:
Family and true love are under siege**

* * *

**If you're on Twitter, tell us what you
think of Harlequin Romantic Suspense!
#harlequinromsuspense**

Dear Reader,

Six years ago, Wyatt Colton's wife, Bailey, left him without any warning. Shortly after that, divorce papers arrived in the mail, signaling an end to a marriage that he had thought was going fine. It took him a long time to get over her and get on with his life—not an easy feat when his own father was just waiting for him to fail and come back to the fold to take over the family "empire." Then, just as suddenly as she left, Bailey turns up on Wyatt's doorstep, asking a stunned Wyatt for a favor. She doesn't want to get back together or pick up where they left off. What Bailey wants from her stoic ex-husband is a baby. Because of health issues, time is running out for Bailey and the situation is "now or never" as far as having a baby is concerned. Wyatt is, and always was, the best man she has ever known, which is why she wants him to father her child.

Will he say yes, or will he send her packing after all the damage she has done to his heart and his self-esteem? Come, read and find out how he reconciles his pain with what he does next.

As always, I thank you for taking the time to read one of my stories, and from the very bottom of my heart, I wish you someone to love who loves you back.

All the best,

Marie Ferrarella

COLTON COWBOY STANDOFF

Marie Ferrarella

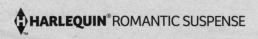

HARLEQUIN® ROMANTIC SUSPENSE

If you purchased this book without a cover you should be aware that this book is stolen property. It was reported as "unsold and destroyed" to the publisher, and neither the author nor the publisher has received any payment for this "stripped book."

Special thanks and acknowledgment are given to Marie Ferrarella for her contribution to The Coltons of Roaring Springs miniseries.

ISBN-13: 978-1-335-66181-4

Colton Cowboy Standoff

Copyright © 2018 by Harlequin Books S.A.

Recycling programs for this product may not exist in your area.

All rights reserved. Except for use in any review, the reproduction or utilization of this work in whole or in part in any form by any electronic, mechanical or other means, now known or hereafter invented, including xerography, photocopying and recording, or in any information storage or retrieval system, is forbidden without the written permission of the publisher, Harlequin Enterprises Limited, 22 Adelaide St. West, 40th Floor, Toronto, Ontario M5H 4E3, Canada.

This is a work of fiction. Names, characters, places and incidents are either the product of the author's imagination or are used fictitiously, and any resemblance to actual persons, living or dead, business establishments, events or locales is entirely coincidental.

This edition published by arrangement with Harlequin Books S.A.

For questions and comments about the quality of this book, please contact us at CustomerService@Harlequin.com.

® and TM are trademarks of Harlequin Enterprises Limited or its corporate affiliates. Trademarks indicated with ® are registered in the United States Patent and Trademark Office, the Canadian Intellectual Property Office and in other countries.

Printed in U.S.A.

™ www.Harlequin.com

USA TODAY bestselling and RITA® Award–winning author **Marie Ferrarella** has written more than two hundred and fifty books for Harlequin, some under the name Marie Nicole. Her romances are beloved by fans worldwide. Visit her website, marieferrarella.com.

Books by Marie Ferrarella

Harlequin Romantic Suspense

The Coltons of Roaring Springs

Colton Cowboy Standoff

Top Secret Deliveries

Cavanaugh's Secret Delivery

Cavanaugh Justice

Mission: Cavanaugh Baby
Cavanaugh on Duty
A Widow's Guilty Secret
Cavanaugh's Surrender
Cavanaugh Rules
Cavanaugh's Bodyguard
Cavanaugh Fortune
How to Seduce a Cavanaugh
Cavanaugh or Death
Cavanaugh Cold Case
Cavanaugh in the Rough
Cavanaugh on Call
Cavanaugh Encounter
Cavanaugh Vanguard

The Coltons of Red Ridge

Colton Baby Rescue

Visit the Author Profile page at
Harlequin.com for more titles.

To

Every couple

Who had their hearts set on a baby

And found that the path was not always that easy.

Chapter 1

"Hello, Wyatt. How are you?"

The woman's low, melodic voice hypnotically wove its way into his bloodstream.

Wyatt Colton stood in the doorway of the Crooked C ranch house, completely speechless and trying to remember if he'd somehow gotten drunk last night without having any memory of it.

But he knew he hadn't.

He'd cleaned up his act several years back, substituting work to numb himself instead and to blanket the hurt he'd felt when she'd left him. Last night, like so many other nights, he'd been dead tired and had just fallen into bed, still dressed with his boots on.

The same way he'd woken up this morning.

But a hallucination was the only way he could

explain why he was suddenly seeing Bailey, tall, golden-brown-haired and beautiful, standing on his porch, talking to him as if it was just any other day.

As if nothing had ever happened.

As if she hadn't ripped his heart out of his chest, breaking it into a million pieces when she'd suddenly walked out on him and on their marriage without giving him even a single warning regarding her intentions.

He felt as if he'd been torpedoed when the divorce papers had arrived in the mail.

"Stunned," Wyatt finally said, answering his ex-wife's question when he was finally able to find his tongue and get it to work.

His tongue might be working but his brain was another story.

The first year after Bailey had left, he'd kept fantasizing about situations like this one. Scenarios in which he would open his front door—the door of the ranch house they had begun to build together—and find Bailey standing there. Sometimes repentant and contrite, other times smiling through tears, but always telling him that she'd been wrong to leave him. The scenarios would always end with Bailey throwing her arms around his neck and him forgiving her as he lost himself in the sweet taste of her lips.

As time went on, the fantasies occurred less and less frequently until he was finally able to make it through a whole month without aching for her.

Well, almost.

However, the pain did ease up and he felt he was almost human again...

And now here she was, standing in front of him, in the flesh, and Wyatt found himself suddenly catapulted back to the shaken shell of the man he'd been right after Bailey had left him.

Staring at her now, he couldn't help thinking she looked almost shy standing there. As if she didn't know what seeing her like this was doing to him.

"May I come in?" Bailey asked in a quiet voice, shifting and feeling somewhat awkward standing there on the front porch.

Her fingertips were cold, colder than even the Colorado January air warranted. Wyatt looked almost like a stranger, not at all like the man she had loved and lived with six years ago. His shaggy, dark brown hair, bits of gray just coming in at the temples, framed dark blue eyes and a left cheek with a slight hint of a dimple.

Had she made a mistake, coming back? Was he going to turn her away after all?

For a moment it seemed as if Wyatt wasn't going to answer her question. And then, when he opened his mouth, she could feel her heart squeeze in fear, afraid that he would say no and then close the door on her.

So when Wyatt finally said, "Sure," and stepped back to allow her access into the house, Bailey felt the corners of her eyes growing moist.

Willing her tears not to fall, she walked into the wide, warm, inviting living room.

"I like what you've done with the place," she told him after a beat. She slowly looked around and took in the room in its entirety.

Initially they had worked on this room together but hadn't gotten nearly finished when she'd suddenly taken off.

It all came flooding back to him, every detail, every feeling, as if it had been just yesterday.

"It needed furniture," he told Bailey with a careless shrug.

Bailey looked around again, taking more in. They had only finished building half the ranch house before she'd made her mind up to leave.

"Well, you did a nice job, Wyatt," she murmured and then added, "Really," in case he thought she was just mouthing empty words.

Wyatt frowned. His guard was up, but even so he could feel her getting to him.

She always could.

His resolve kicked in. He wasn't going to allow himself to be set up for another bout of mind-numbing disappointment, he thought fiercely. He'd barely survived the last time and had just gotten to the point where he was breathing regularly.

He couldn't go through all that again.

He wouldn't be able to survive it.

His dark blue eyes narrowed as he looked at the

woman he had believed would be by his side forever. The joke was on him, he thought bitterly.

In the beginning it seemed as if Fate had purposely thrown them together when he'd left home and embarked on making a name for himself outside the oppressive Colton sphere of interest.

All of his life he'd been overshadowed by his family and his last name. When his father, Russ, wouldn't allow him to do what he'd wanted to do—insisting instead that his oldest son get a business degree so he could take over the family business—Wyatt had abruptly dropped out of college, left his family and taken to the road.

His father had all but gone into a rage when he'd learned that his firstborn was following the rodeo circuit.

It was on that same circuit that Wyatt had met Bailey-Ann Norton.

A rodeo brat whose father took her with him as he went from town to town, following the circuit, Bailey had never known another life. Eventually she'd become a barrel racer.

Their attraction was immediate and strong, but she hadn't thought there was any serious commitment on his part. That hadn't happened until Wyatt had learned his beloved grandmother had died, leaving him a sizable amount of land right outside of Roaring Springs, Colorado.

It seemed like an omen, the next step in his desire to make something of himself apart from his father's almighty influence. Tired of the aches and pains he'd accumulated as a bull rider, Wyatt decided to change his plans—again. He'd asked Bailey to marry him and help him create a home and a ranch.

He remembered that Bailey had never looked more beautiful than when she had smiled up at him and cried, "Yes!"

They'd returned to Roaring Springs and started building their home and the ranch he envisioned.

He'd thought things were going well. Obviously he'd thought wrong. A few years into their marriage, Bailey had suddenly left him.

Wyatt felt as if he'd been gut-shot.

It had taken him all this time to get over her, to get on with his life and finally become whole again.

And now she was back!

Why was she here?

It made no sense to him.

He wanted to know. "Did you come back here just to give the place a once-over?" he snapped, a cold edge in his voice.

Bailey's courage almost failed her then. But she had come this far—she couldn't just back out now. She had to tell him why she'd sought him out after all this time.

"No," she answered Wyatt quietly, "that's not why I'm here."

"Then why *are* you here, Bailey?" he demanded.

Bailey took a deep breath, hoping her voice wouldn't crack. She raised her head slightly, doing her best to look and sound as if she was in command of herself, in command of the moment. She knew that her ex-husband didn't like displays of weakness. He valued bravery, even in an enemy, which she knew was the way he probably thought of her. At least to start with.

Her dark eyes met his.

You've got this, Bailey, she told herself. Her voice sounded as if it was echoing in her head as she answered his question.

"I'm here because I want to have a baby and I want you to be the father."

Chapter 2

His eyes might not be playing tricks on him but his ears had to be, Wyatt thought. He couldn't have heard what he *thought* he'd just heard.

"Say what now?" he asked, unabashedly staring at Bailey.

Wyatt vaguely remembered that when they'd first gotten married they had discussed having children, but they had decided it would be best to wait a few years. At the time he'd felt their energy had to be focused on making a go of the ranch. But, he remembered thinking, they would have plenty of time for kids later.

The subject had never come up again. In the beginning they'd been too busy with the house and the ranch, and then, when there might have been a better time to start a family, Bailey had taken off.

"A baby," she repeated, her eyes on his. "I want to have a baby, and whatever our differences might be, I still think that you're the best man I ever knew and I want you to be the father."

Wyatt was attempting to process the words he had just heard. Moving like a man who couldn't quite feel his legs, he walked farther into the sprawling living room and sank onto the comfortably worn leather sofa. Once sitting, he indicated that Bailey should sit on the sofa, as well.

When she did, only then did he speak.

"Just like that?" Wyatt asked her, astonished. "I don't hear from you for six years and then you walk back into my life, telling me you want me to be the father of your *baby*?" Even as he said the words out loud he couldn't quite believe this was happening. Bailey had always been so levelheaded, so sensible, and this was a totally irrational request. "Why?" He wanted to know. "Isn't there anyone else around?" he demanded.

"I don't want just 'anyone,'" Bailey told him softly. "I want you."

It couldn't be as simple as that. There had to be something more to it, he thought. Something she wasn't telling him. He frowned. "Assuming I believe you—"

"You should," Bailey interjected. Why would he think she was lying? She'd never lied to him before, she thought defensively.

"*Assuming* I believe you," Wyatt deliberately repeated. "Why a baby now, all of a sudden?"

Bailey took a breath before answering. She supposed he had a right to know.

None of this, including coming out here, had been easy for her. She wasn't the type who asked for favors. On the contrary, she had always gone out and gotten whatever she wanted or needed all by herself.

But this time was different. This time she couldn't be the lone wolf. She needed help.

"Because I'm running out of time," Bailey confessed.

That was twice he'd been caught off guard in the space of less than ten minutes.

"You're dying?" Wyatt asked in a hushed, stunned voice as he stared at her in disbelief. Bailey had always been so bright, so lively. He couldn't begin to imagine her being felled by some sort of terminal disease.

"No," Bailey quickly answered, wanting to correct any misimpression he might have gotten. "I'm not dying. But my chances of getting pregnant are."

She looked pretty healthy to him, Wyatt thought, confused. He shook his head. "I don't understand."

Why couldn't he just say yes to her request? Why did he need this all spelled out for him?

"This isn't easy for me to talk about," Bailey told him, wanting to beg off from making any elaborate explanations.

"Take your time," he told her. "You came out all

this way to talk to a man you turned your back on, so this has to be important to you," he surmised, waiting for her to speak up.

Bailey didn't know if he was being incredibly sensitive or if he was just being sarcastic. Either way, she knew she was going to have to ride this out and answer his question. Wyatt was her only hope and that meant she had to make him understand so that he would agree to father this baby.

Taking a deep breath, she plunged into the explanation she was afraid he would find as embarrassing as she did. Or at the very least, confusing.

But there was no way around it.

"My cycles have always been inconsistent…" she began, her throat feeling particularly dry.

"Cycles?" Wyatt questioned, not really sure what she was talking about.

Okay, she'd state it another way, Bailey thought, still trying to be delicate about her explanation. "My time of the month."

The light suddenly dawned on Wyatt. "Oh." He avoided her eyes as he said, "Go on."

She started to get more technical. It felt somehow less embarrassing that way. "I found out that was caused by polycystic ovarian syndrome."

"Okay," he said only because he wanted her to get on with it so that they could get to the end of all this. He was a horse breeder and didn't understand terms that weren't directly involved with the care and breeding of his herd.

She could tell by the way Wyatt had just said "okay" that he didn't understand what she was telling him. Bailey tried again. "Because of that condition—it's called PCOS—my getting pregnant becomes harder and harder the older I get."

"You're just in your midthirties," Wyatt pointed out.

She took that to mean that she'd finally gotten through to him and he was starting to understand her dilemma.

"Exactly," she cried, nodding her head. "That means it's now or never if I want to have a baby."

Bailey searched his face to see if Wyatt was still following her or if he'd lost interest. But he looked as if he was waiting for her to go on. So, taking heart, Bailey continued, doing her best to play on his sympathies.

"I have wanted a child of my own ever since I was a kid. A child I could love. A child I could give the kind of emotional support and material things to that I never had when I was growing up." She paused for a moment, turning on the sofa to look into his eyes. To appeal to him. "But I need you to make that happen."

Wyatt was having trouble wrapping his head around what she was telling him. He kept coming back to the fact that she was the one who had walked out on him, not the other way around. She was the one who had sent the divorce papers. She'd obviously wanted nothing more to do with him then, and now here she was, asking him to make a baby with her.

It just didn't add up.

"What changed your mind?" He measured out the words slowly.

He'd lost her. "I don't understand," she told him.

"Well, you didn't seem to want to stay with me six years ago," Wyatt reminded her, "so what's changed?"

"Nothing." That wasn't strictly true, she thought, so she rephrased her statement. "At least, not my opinion of you," she amended. Because she could see that she'd managed to further confuse him, Bailey tried again. "I didn't marry you because you were a Colton or because you'd suddenly inherited your own ranch. I married you because you were a good, decent man."

He waited for that to make sense to him. When it didn't, he asked, "If that's true, if that's how you felt, why did you leave?"

Bailey shook her head. There was no point in going into all that now. She wasn't here to fix a broken marriage with a man she couldn't forget. She was here to try to salvage something for her future.

"That's complicated."

"And yet you thought it was worthwhile to come back," he said, mystified.

And then she realized why he was confused, why he was holding back.

"I came back just to get pregnant," she explained. "I'm not planning on staying once that happens," she assured him, thinking he was worried he was going to be saddled with her, at least until the pregnancy was over. "You don't have to worry. I'll be out of your hair the moment I know that you were success-ful getting me pregnant."

"Even breeding horses involves more romance than this," Wyatt told her.

"I'm not looking for anything from you except your 'donation,'" Bailey said, trying to get her point across to him while attempting to resist his sexy gaze. "You won't be on the hook for child support or any sort of money at all. Really," she emphasized.

Wyatt looked as if he had his doubts about what she'd just said. "If that's the case, just how do you plan on taking care of this baby if and when I say yes and you do get pregnant?"

"I can take care of us," Bailey answered.

"I asked you how," Wyatt repeated, still waiting for a concrete answer that made sense to him.

She hadn't planned on opening up her life to him once again, but now it seemed that she had to…but she refused to let him break her heart again.

"Do you remember when I told you I wanted to become a veterinarian?" she asked.

It had been one of the reasons why she'd finally left him. Because becoming a veterinarian had always been a dream of hers and he had asked her to put it on hold for him until after they got the ranch up and running.

Just as he'd asked her to hold off on having babies. Everything she'd wanted, everything that had meant anything to her, he'd asked her to put on hold—until she felt as if *all* of her was on hold in deference to him.

"Judging from the look on your face, you don't remember," Bailey concluded. "Well, I did it." She saw him raise a quizzical eyebrow. He still wasn't following her, she thought. "I became one," she told him. "I became a veterinarian and started up a small practice of my own. That means that I'll be able to pay for this baby when he or she arrives."

Bailey took a breath then continued. "So, as I said, all I need from you is your 'donation.'" She held her breath as she nervously searched his face. "What do you say?"

Wyatt remained silent for a while, as if honestly considering her question and thinking it over. But when he spoke, it wasn't to give her an answer, positive or otherwise.

"I don't know, Bailey," he told her. "This is a big decision."

"It doesn't have to be," she pointed out, trying not to sound as frustrated as she felt. She hadn't come all this way to hear him turn her down. "Men have one-night stands all the time. You could think of it that way. Or you could think of it as making love to an old girlfriend for old times' sake."

"But you weren't my girlfriend," Wyatt pointed out, his eyes narrowing. "You were my wife."

Bailey shrugged, shoving down the emotions threatening to overwhelm her. "Same thing."

Wyatt shook his head. "Not really. There's a big difference."

She squared her shoulders, bracing herself for the

answer she didn't want from the man she'd never forgotten. "So it's no?" she asked, too disappointed to try to hide her reaction.

"No, it's not no…" he began.

"Then it's yes?" she asked excitedly.

"It's not that, either," he told her before she could get carried away, although he hated seeing that light in her eyes go out. It reminded him of the way things used to be when they were first married and anything seemed possible. "I already said that I'll have to give this some thought," he explained. "Getting together to create a baby is a big step."

"I know. That's why I'm asking you," she stressed. "I told you, you're the best man I know."

One of them had to be logical, he thought. It didn't look like it was going to be her, so he'd been elected.

"Flattering as that is, I wouldn't be such a 'best man' if I just jumped right into this without considering all the ramifications," he told her.

"There aren't any," Bailey insisted. How did she get that across to him? She felt desperate. He had to say yes.

"I'm afraid I'd have to disagree with you," Wyatt told her. "This would be a little person we'd be bringing into the world."

"A little person you wouldn't be required to do anything for," she reminded him again.

Maybe if he approached this a different way. "You came to me, right?"

Bailey blew out a breath. "Obviously."

"Why?"

She closed her eyes, struggling to keep her emotions in check. "I already told you. I came to you because you are the only person I want to be the father of my child."

He nodded. "I'm assuming that has something to do with my character."

"Obviously," she agreed, wondering where he was going with this.

"Well, this is part of my character. I'm not jumping right into this. I have to think about it," Wyatt told her.

Bailey knew that look. She could see that there was no talking him out of this. His mind was made up. Sighing, she surrendered. "All right," she said. "How long are you going to think about it?"

"Until I make up my mind," Wyatt answered evasively.

She'd meant it when she'd said she wanted him for her baby's father. That meant that she had to go along with him in this.

"Looks like I'm going to be here for a while, then." She hadn't planned on this. "I guess I should have made my reservation at the Lodge for a longer period of time," Bailey added, mentioning one of the Colton family's enterprises. "I just booked it for a couple of days."

This was going to be difficult, Wyatt thought. But he'd meant it when he'd said he needed time to mull this over.

There was only one option left open to him.

"No need," he told her. "You're welcome to stay here."

"Here?" Bailey repeated, stunned. She looked around then back at Wyatt. "With you?"

He nodded. "If you're here, it'll help me make up my mind that much quicker," he told her. "And with you here, we can use the time to catch up." His eyes narrowed slightly as he looked at Bailey. "Unless you have something to hide."

She stared at him, completely taken aback. "Why would you say something like that?"

She had to ask? "Because I don't hear a word from you for six years." And in the beginning, he'd sought comfort in the bottom of a bottle, convinced that he'd never get over her running out on him like that. Recovery had been slower than he'd ever thought possible. But he'd done it—and he didn't want to risk a relapse. "Not so much as a phone call or a postcard, and then you show up out of the blue, asking me to father your baby. You have to admit that would make anyone leery."

"Maybe if that person didn't know me," Bailey pointed out. "You know me."

"Do I?" he quipped. "I thought I did. But the woman I knew wouldn't have just taken off without a word of explanation the way you did. Which means I didn't really know you at all," he emphasized.

Bailey sighed again. Maybe she should extend

an olive branch and explain a bit more. To the man she'd once loved.

"I left because I was losing my identity," she told him.

He scowled. "What does that even mean?"

"It means that you put everything ahead of me. I wanted to become a veterinarian. You told me to hold off on that until after we get the ranch up and running. So I said all right and I held off. I wanted kids. You said okay, but you wanted us to wait until after we finished building the house. So again I said okay. But it *wasn't* okay. Not really. I was giving up bits and pieces of me until I didn't even recognize myself."

Wyatt frowned. "So you left."

There was no way she could argue the point. "I had to."

"And those vows you took? The ones about loving me until death do us part? Those didn't mean enough to you to make you stay?" he bit out.

Her answer, if it was truthful, surprised him.

"Those meant *everything* to me," she insisted.

"But you left anyway."

"I left *because* of them," she insisted. "Don't you see?"

Baffled, Wyatt shook his head. "No, I don't."

"If I'd stayed, I would have wound up resenting you because you were stifling me," she told him. "Not intentionally, I know that now, but the result was the same. I was losing my sense of who I was, other than

just the woman by your side, the one who was helping you build this big ranch house while taking myself apart. Eventually, I knew I was going to wind up
hating you for what was happening to me."

"So you left."

"I had to. I had to sacrifice our marriage in order
to save the feelings we had for each other," Bailey insisted.

That made absolutely no sense to him. "I don't
understand."

She smiled. "I don't expect you to," she told Wyatt
wistfully. "But just know that I always loved you.
And I always will."

Chapter 3

Bailey had managed to catch him off guard again. Wyatt had lost count of how many times that made since he'd opened his door this morning.

But just know that I always loved you. And I always will.

Her words echoed in his head. Wyatt frowned. Was his ex-wife just playing him, professing that she felt something for him as a means to an end?

"Don't say things you don't mean," he retorted, growing angry. "It's not going to propel me to make up my mind any faster."

Bailey tried not to take offense at being dismissed this way. She had hurt him and that cut him a lot of slack in her opinion. But he should have known better.

"I didn't say it for that reason and I *don't* say things I don't mean," Bailey reminded him tersely.

She rose to her feet and began walking toward the door.

Wyatt was right behind her. "Where are you going?"

"I'm going for a drive to clear my head—and to cancel my reservation at the Lodge," she answered. As quickly as it had threatened to flare up, her temper had receded again. Her voice softened as she told him, "I'll be back later. You still keep your doors unlocked?"

"Yes." Roaring Springs was a relatively small community and trust was a way of life here. For the most part, neighbors all looked out for one another.

Bailey nodded. She thought so. "Good. Then I'll let myself in when I get back." About to open the door and leave, she stopped as something else suddenly occurred to her. Turning back, she looked at Wyatt as she asked, "You're not with anyone, are you? I mean, I won't be walking in on your girlfriend or mistress or significant other when I come back to the ranch, will I?" Her eyes washed over his face, searching for an answer.

"A little late to be asking that, isn't it?" Wyatt retorted, somewhat amused by her question. In the last six years there'd been no one who'd even remotely stirred his interest—especially the way Bailey had. As far as he was concerned, that part of his life was over.

The slightest hint of color rose to her cheeks. Wyatt

was right. It hadn't occurred to her until just this moment that he might have moved on. She hadn't, so she'd just assumed he hadn't, either. Was he making fun of her? Or was this his subtle way of hinting that he actually *was* involved with someone else.

She avoided his eyes as she told him, "I didn't exactly rehearse any of this beforehand."

"That's obvious," he commented. And then he took pity on her. Embarrassing Bailey didn't make him feel any better about what had gone down between them. "And no, there's no girlfriend or mistress or significant other to worry about."

"No one?" Bailey asked, wanting to be absolutely sure he was being honest.

He caught the note of suspicion in her voice. "Why? Would you feel better if there was?" Wyatt asked, interpreting her question to mean she was worried once she got what she had come for, he might try to make her stay.

But he had no such intentions. He was neither a masochist nor a slow learner. Being unceremoniously dumped once was more than enough for him. He had no desire to suffer through that again. His heart didn't need to be cut out of his chest a second time.

"No," Bailey quickly denied. "I just wanted to make sure that I wouldn't accidentally mess up your relationship."

His eyes met hers. "Once was enough," he told her in a cold voice.

Bailey had no idea how to respond to that. At the

time, she hadn't thought she mattered all that much to him. She quite honestly didn't even think he'd notice she was gone immediately because he was so fixated on building up the ranch to the exclusion of everything else. Other than representing another pair of hands he could call on, she could have been anyone.

For a moment she debated apologizing, telling him she was sorry. But she really wasn't sorry. Because if she hadn't left, she would have never become a veterinarian, never become her own person.

For now, she decided it was best just to leave the subject alone.

"I'll be back later," she repeated as she started to leave again. Pausing, she added, "And thank you for hearing me out."

"I haven't said yes yet," he reminded her, following her to the front door.

"I know. One step at a time."

Opening the door, she walked out just as a tall, lean, muscular cowboy was coming up the walk. Their eyes met for a split second, and then Bailey lowered hers and hurried off to where she had parked her car.

Foxworth Colton's mouth dropped open as the woman registered belatedly in his brain. Like a cartoon character, Wyatt's cousin/adopted brother turned around and watched the woman he had almost walked into quickly get into her car and drive away.

Still stunned, Fox turned back to look quizzically at Wyatt.

Harrison Colton, Fox's father, had died following

a deadly accident where he'd unintentionally driven his car off the road. Fox's mother, Dana, who'd been in the passenger seat, had lingered long enough to ask her sister, Mara, to care for her children. Wyatt's parents had both agreed to take in Fox and Sloane.

Because they were close and always had been, when Wyatt had inherited the Crooked C from his grandmother, he'd set aside forty acres on the southern part of his property and offered it to Fox so that his cousin was able to breed his horses. In return Fox worked closely with Wyatt and could always be called upon to help out when Wyatt needed him.

No one had been happier for Wyatt than Fox when Wyatt had gotten married. Fox had also been there for him when Bailey had suddenly taken off for parts unknown. Fox had been the one to slowly ease Wyatt away from trying to drown his pain in alcohol when that process threatened to get the better of him.

Fox's patience and efforts had paid off. Wyatt had finally gotten back to his old self, albeit more closed off emotionally than he'd been previously.

But that could all change again with Bailey coming back, Fox thought.

Maybe he was mistaken. Maybe that only *looked* like Bailey. After all, why would she suddenly come back after all this time?

"Hey," Fox said, doing his best to sound cheerful, "that wasn't— ?"

"Bailey?" Wyatt supplied. Turning on his heel,

he walked away from the front door. His voice was flat as he answered, "Yes, it was."

Bordering on shocked disbelief, Fox walked into the house right behind Wyatt. He glanced over his shoulder one last time even though the car and the woman were gone. "You're kidding."

"Not something I'd kid about," Wyatt assured the younger man.

Fox closed the door behind him and went straight to the coffee maker on the kitchen counter. He needed a hit of coffee, the stronger the better.

"What's she doing here?" Taking a mug from the counter, he filled it to the brim with inky-black coffee. "Did she suddenly come to her senses?" he asked even though he doubted that was why Bailey had suddenly turned up.

"I don't think that's why she's here."

Fox looked at the man above the rim of steaming black liquid. "Then why *is* she here?" He burned his tongue and swallowed a curse. Blowing on the liquid, he waited a second before taking another sip, slowly this time.

"She came to ask if I'd make a baby with her."

Fox had just taken another sip of coffee. He started choking and almost spit the liquid out in a spray. He managed to swallow it at the last moment.

He set the mug down on the kitchen counter, and his eyes were watery as he stared at his cousin. "I thought you just said that she asked you—"

"She did," Wyatt said quietly.

Forgetting about the coffee, Fox focused his attention on Wyatt. He didn't want to see the man he thought of as a brother getting hurt again. "When did all this happen?"

Wyatt nodded at the closed front door. "Just now."

That didn't seem possible, Fox thought. "She didn't give you any warning?"

Wyatt shook his head as he walked back into the living room. "Nope."

Fox was right behind him. "You're telling me that Bailey didn't call you first to see how you felt about this?"

Feeling suddenly drained, Wyatt sank onto the sofa. The same sofa he had just been sitting on with Bailey beside him. It almost seemed like a crazy dream now.

"That's what I'm telling you."

Fox was trying to get this all straight in his head. "And you haven't heard from her in the last six years, right?"

Wyatt's eyes shifted, slowly looking toward his brother. "Not a word."

Fox emitted a low whistle. "Hell, Wyatt, what are you going to do?"

Wyatt laughed even though the situation was far from funny. "Damned if I know."

Fox's mind was racing now. "She's not staying in town, is she?"

The corners of Wyatt's mouth rose in an ironic smile. "As a matter of fact, she isn't."

Fox looked at his cousin suspiciously. "I don't like the way you phrased that." And then it hit him. "Wait—she's not staying here, is she? *Please* tell me she's not staying here."

"I could," Wyatt answered, "except that I made it a point never to lie to you."

Astonishment nudged its way into Fox's soul. "She's going to be staying here," he concluded incredulously. He stared at Wyatt, unable to believe what the other man was telling him. Maybe there was some mistake. "You're actually considering doing what she asked?"

"Well, I—"

Wyatt got no further than that before Fox barked, "Wyatt, are you out of your mind? This woman did a tap dance on your heart, disappearing on you without even having the decency to tell you why to your face, and now she's popped up out of nowhere, asking you to sleep with her—"

Maybe it was nerves that made Wyatt laugh at the way Fox was phrasing his narrative. "Actually, sleeping isn't exactly a factor here—"

Fox wasn't in the mood to see the humor in this. "You know damn well what I mean. Maybe you don't remember what you were like after she left because most of the time you were too anesthetized with whiskey to know your own name. But *I* remember the whole thing. Clearly," he emphasized. "She practically destroyed you—and I'm not going to let her get a chance to do it a second time," Fox informed him angrily.

Wyatt knew that the other man meant well, but

this was his problem to deal with. "You don't have anything to say about it."

"The hell I don't," Fox snapped. "For better or for worse, you're my family and I care about you. Now you might not be able to say no to that woman, but I certainly can," Fox informed him with finality.

Wyatt raised a salient point. "She didn't ask you to father her baby, Fox. She asked me."

Fox scowled. He was incensed and didn't like being tripped up because of words. "You know what I mean," he growled.

"Yeah, I do," Wyatt replied. And then his voice softened. "And I know you mean well but, ultimately, this is my decision to make."

"So you're *actually* considering doing this?"

"I'm *thinking* about it," Wyatt corrected him. To him thinking came before considering and he needed to think this all through, taking in all the ramifications, the extenuating circumstances as far as he was able. "Look, I'm the one who brought her out here and she sacrificed a lot to help me get the ranch up and running. I owe her."

"Is that what she told you?" Fox chided angrily. "That you owe her?"

"No, that's what *I* think. And it's true. Bailey wanted to go to school to become a veterinarian and I talked her out of it, saying she could do that later because I needed her working alongside me at the time.

"I said the same thing to her when she wanted to have kids." Wyatt went on, vividly remembering the circumstances now. "I said having kids could wait because we needed to focus our attention on the ranch and getting a herd going."

Fox refused to allow Wyatt to blame himself. "So you wanted to build something and you did. That wasn't a bad thing," he insisted.

"No, it wasn't," Wyatt agreed. "But it wasn't *her* thing," he said, trying to see the situation from his ex-wife's vantage point. "It was mine. Bailey didn't get to do what she wanted, didn't get to have the kids she wanted."

"So she's here to collect now?" Fox asked in astonishment. "Is that what you're saying?"

Wyatt frowned to himself as he sighed. There were so many ambivalent feelings running through him. "Something like that."

This still wasn't making any sense to Fox. "Bailey's still young," he insisted. "She's what? Thirty? Thirty-one?"

"Thirty-five," Wyatt corrected him.

"Thirty-five," Fox repeated, nodding his head as if this substantiated the point he was about to make. "Not exactly ready for the old age home. Plenty of time for her to have a baby." He paused, looking at his cousin. "No offense, but why you? It's been six years. She should have moved on."

Wyatt shrugged. "I don't know," he said. "She said I was the best man she knew."

"She joined a convent after she left you?" Fox wanted to know, keeping a straight face.

"Very funny," Wyatt retorted. "No, apparently she made a discerning decision."

Fox grew serious. "All kidding aside, Wyatt, you *are* the best man I've ever known, but even taking that into account, you could be letting yourself in for a lot of grief here." He was silent for a moment, thinking. "Maybe she has an agenda, coming back to you after all this time."

Wyatt had come a long way from the man he had been six years ago. That man had felt he'd had something to prove to his parents by making a success of himself. He was less driven now. Even so, it felt as if there was something still missing from his life. Maybe this was it. He didn't know, but it was worth thinking about. "Like what?" he asked Fox.

"Your last name is Colton," Fox reminded Wyatt. "She has your baby, she has a claim on the Colton money."

Wyatt shook his head. "No, she said she didn't want anything from me except my DNA."

"Women say a lot of things to get their way," Fox pointed out.

That might be so in some cases, but he'd believed Bailey when she'd said she wanted nothing from him. "When those divorce papers arrived in the mail, she never asked me to do anything but sign them. There was no settlement in her favor, no requests for alimony made. I was a Colton then, too," he reminded Fox.

His cousin wasn't altogether convinced. "Maybe

she's gotten smarter since then and realized she missed a huge opportunity."

"Fox, you've met her. In some respects, you knew her almost as well as I did," Wyatt argued. "Does that sound like the woman you knew?"

Wyatt had a point, Fox acknowledged. But he still thought Wyatt should hold off just in case. "People change, Wyatt."

"*People* change." Wyatt emphasized the word. "Bailey hasn't. And she went back to school just like she wanted to. She got her degree and became a veterinarian," he told Fox, realizing that a bit of pride had slipped into his voice as he'd told his cousin about his ex-wife's accomplishment.

Fox studied Wyatt's face in silence for a long moment. And then he nodded his head, not in response to anything the other man had said, but in response to something that had just occurred to him.

"You've made up your mind, haven't you?" he asked. "You're going to tell her yes."

But Wyatt wasn't all that quick to confirm his cousin's assumption. Instead he said, "Right now, I'm leaning that way."

"Think long and hard, Wyatt," Fox counseled. "Truth be told, until she stomped on your heart, I always liked Bailey. I thought she was good for you. But think about this… If you say yes and she has this baby, how are you going to feel when she takes it away? That's what she said, right? That all she wants is your DNA and then she's gone.

"I know you, Wyatt," Fox told him. "You father that baby, you're going to want to be part of its life and maybe Bailey won't want that. Maybe she'll just pull another disappearing act on you when you're not looking, and this time, she'll be running off with your son or your daughter. How are you going to feel then?"

"You're asking too many questions," Wyatt said dismissively.

"And you're not asking enough," Fox insisted. "You might have a big heart and be a pushover when it comes to Bailey, but I'm here to make sure that you're not hurt again."

Wyatt looked at his cousin impatiently. "I can take care of myself."

Fox didn't see it that way. "Obviously not."

"I haven't said yes yet," Wyatt reminded him, hoping that would shut Fox up for the time being.

"But you're going to, aren't you?" he asked. It was a rhetorical question.

Wyatt cocked his head and pretended to listen to something in the distance. "I think I hear the horses calling you."

For now, Fox gave up. They both needed a little space to allow this to settle. "We're not finished talking yet. This isn't over. In the meantime, I'm going to confiscate the alcohol you keep here."

Wyatt knew what his brother was referring to. It wasn't a period of his life he was proud of. "You don't have to worry. I'm not about to make the same mistake twice," he told Fox.

Fox paused by the front door. "Just remember that you said that," he said before he left.

Chapter 4

Working alongside Fox today, Wyatt found that he had spent a good part of the time defending Bailey. He'd had no idea that Fox had so many misgivings about his former wife's sudden reappearance. More, apparently, than he did.

Wyatt was well aware where his brother was coming from. Most likely, in Fox's position, he might even feel the same way. But from somewhere deep within him, something akin to a sense of protectiveness stirred inside Wyatt. Right or wrong, he felt compelled to get Fox to change his mind, or at the very least to hold off making any final judgments against Bailey until she'd had a chance to redeem herself.

But after going back and forth for the length of

the day, at the end of that time they were still at an impasse and Wyatt left it at that. Especially since he really hadn't made up his mind one way or the other regarding Bailey's request.

Preoccupied, Wyatt didn't notice the car that was parked around the side of the ranch house until he had already walked inside. That was when the combined scent of chicken frying in the pan mingled with the light perfume she always wore seeped into his consciousness.

Bailey had returned.

Suddenly all the old, angry feelings came rushing back to him, fast and hard, like a river overflowing its banks, practically drowning him.

Wyatt forgot about all the things he had said to Fox in her defense, remembering instead the sickening, hollow feeling in his gut when he'd realized that she was really gone.

Walking into the kitchen, he saw Bailey moving between the counter and the stove, her back to him. For a second he thought of turning around and storming out, but that wouldn't solve anything. She was there and he was going to have to deal with it.

"You made dinner," Wyatt observed, coming up behind her.

Startled, Bailey nearly dropped the frying pan she'd just lifted from the burner. At the last minute she managed to hold on to it and shift it onto one of the other burners that hadn't been turned on.

Catching her breath, she turned to look at Wyatt over her shoulder.

"Well, I thought you might be hungry when you came home after working on the range, so I looked through the refrigerator to see if there was anything I could use to make dinner." She turned around to face him and smiled. "If I remember correctly, you have a weakness for fried chicken."

He'd once had a weakness for her, as well, Wyatt thought.

"I like it," he replied with a measure of indifference that sounded downright chilly to Bailey.

She tried not to let him see her reaction to his tone. Instead she smiled again then went back to getting everything ready.

"Good, because dinner's almost ready."

The scene was all too familiar to him, vividly bringing back the early days of their marriage when they had worked alongside each other and then taken all their meals together.

"You didn't have to do this," he told her gruffly.

In her estimation, Wyatt looked as if he wished she hadn't, but Bailey ignored that.

"I could say the same thing to you about letting me stay here," she replied, transferring the side dishes from their pots to serving bowls. The bowls were the same ones she'd used when they were together, she noticed. Nothing had changed.

Except that everything had.

Opening the cabinet drawer closest to her, Bailey looked for the set of tongs she thought would be there. But they weren't.

She opened another drawer with the same result. Looking up at Wyatt, she asked, "Where are the tongs?"

Coming up behind her, he looked over her shoulder into the drawer, as if he expected them to suddenly materialize. When he saw they weren't there, Wyatt thought for a minute.

"I think they're in the barn," he told her.

"The barn?" That was an odd place for them. Her brow furrowed beneath her wayward bangs. "What are they doing there?"

Wyatt shrugged. "I needed them for something" was all he said, unable to remember the real reason the tongs had made their way out of the kitchen and into the barn.

Feeling it best not to push the matter or to question him—she'd learned long ago to pick her battles—Bailey merely nodded. "Okay."

Bailey used a fork in lieu of the tongs and put two pieces of chicken on his plate and then one on hers. Picking up both plates, she brought them over to the table, placing one plate in front of Wyatt and one opposite him, where she used to sit. She then got the two bowls, one filled with mashed potatoes and one with green beans, and placed them next to the two plates.

Finished, she sat.

Wyatt took his seat opposite her. He looked down

at her plate critically. "You just took one piece of chicken."

Wyatt started to pick up one of the chicken legs on his plate to transfer to hers but she pulled her plate back from him.

"I was never a big eater," she reminded him, waiting for that information to sink in and ring a bell.

It did. "That's right, I remember. Rosa kept trying to fatten you up, said you were too skinny and you were going to waste away unless she got you to eat more," Wyatt said, referring to his former housekeeper.

Like the property, he had inherited the housekeeper from his grandmother. For just a moment, there was a fond note in his voice as he remembered their first days at the Crooked C.

"Remember how mad she got when it started raining in the kitchen?" Bailey recalled, laughing at the memory. "That was when we found out the roof we'd just finished putting in leaked. Badly. Rosa wanted you to go out right then and there and patch it."

He recalled the incident. "Sometimes I got the impression that she thought we worked for her."

Bailey nodded, laughing again. "She certainly was bossy." When she'd returned this afternoon, it had become obvious to her that the housekeeper no longer lived there. "Whatever happened to her?" she asked.

"Rosa retired three years ago," he told her as he continued eating. "Her daughter's husband was killed in a tractor accident and she needed help raising her three kids, so Rosa left me to become a full-time grandmother."

He remembered how the woman had kept apologizing for leaving him high and dry like that. He'd known at the time that she'd been thinking about Bailey deserting him three years earlier. He'd told the older woman that there were no hard feelings and had even given her a large bonus to help things along with her grandchildren.

"That's too bad," Bailey said, genuinely saddened to hear the woman had left. "I liked her. Who cooks your meals now?" she asked suddenly.

He fielded the question without flinching. "I do."

Bailey stopped eating and looked at him. When they were married, Wyatt couldn't boil water. When he'd been traveling the rodeo circuit, she remembered that he'd taken all his meals at any local restaurant or diner they'd come across.

"You cook?" she asked, not bothering to hide her surprise.

"I can get by," he answered. Saying anything more would be bordering on lying. "Mostly I heat up things out of cans. But I can make eggs," he added.

A warm smile spread from her eyes to her lips. "I guess miracles do happen," she said wryly.

Mesmerized by her smile, Wyatt looked at his ex-wife for a long moment.

"Maybe sometimes," he allowed then looked away.

He was closing up again, Bailey thought sadly. She could see it.

Bailey bit her lower lip. She was never going to get him to agree to go along with her proposition if he closed up. He'd never been particularly outgoing and cheerful, even when things were going well between them, but at least there had been glimmers of joy evident every now and then.

Now what she sensed was a bitterness that hadn't been there before.

Had she done that to him?

Who was she trying to kid? Bailey upbraided herself. Of course she had done this to him. And now it was up to her to do what she could to undo that, to get him to open up again and be the man she had once known. She didn't want him dissolving into a bitter old man, not when he had so much to offer.

"Well, I look forward to sampling some of your cooking," she told him after a beat, not knowing what else to say. Things were awkward between them. That, too, was her fault, she thought.

"We'll see" was all Wyatt said in response.

Several minutes later he looked down at his plate and realized that despite the tension between them, dinner had gone down very easily. If nothing else, he mused, the woman certainly knew how to cook. But then, she always had.

He felt a pang, sitting opposite her like this. It reminded him just how much he'd missed her all these years. And just how angry he'd been that she'd left, even though, theoretically, he now understood why she had done it.

Bailey's voice broke through his ruminations. "What?"

"You're grimacing," she noted. "Was something wrong with the chicken?"

"No, not at all. It was very good actually. You always did know your way around a kitchen."

She'd never thought of it as an accomplishment but rather a necessity.

"I had to," she told him matter-of-factly. When they were together, she hadn't really shared very much about her mother. She hadn't wanted him to feel sorry for her. It no longer mattered now. "My mom left when I was little and my father was even more hopeless in the kitchen than you were."

"I think I resent that," Wyatt quipped with a small hint of a smile.

"It wasn't meant as an insult, just an observation," she told him, not wanting him to think she was trying to belittle him. "I learned to cook because I had to. Old Prairie Dog Pat wasn't about to let me slide," she recalled, referring to her father by the name that everyone in the circuit called him.

Patrick Norton had been a very hard man to love, but she did because he was her father and, for a long time, her only family. From a very young age, she was the one who'd looked after him instead of the other way around. And he'd returned her devotion by finding different ways to belittle her because as she'd grown, she'd looked like the spitting image of the woman who had walked out on him, leaving him with a kid to raise.

Even after she had forged a career for herself as a barrel racer, and then left it all behind her to marry Wyatt, Bailey could still hear her father's voice in her head, telling her that she would never be good enough to be accepted in Wyatt's world. She was acutely aware of how little her father thought of her.

She supposed that, in part, her father was responsible for her ultimately leaving Wyatt. She'd felt she needed to make something of herself so that she could respect herself. Otherwise she'd been certain that no one else ever would, especially Wyatt.

"Anyway," she continued, shutting away the wave of hurtful memories, "I'm sure you've gotten very good at it."

A dry laugh escaped his lips. "Maybe you should reserve judgment on that until after you've had a chance to actually sample my cooking."

That sounded promising to her—on more than one level, she thought. For her to sample his cooking, he had to make it for her. That in turn meant she had to be here for that. In a roundabout way, he was telling her that she was staying.

"I look forward to it," Bailey told him.

"Uh-huh," he murmured, pushing back his chair.

Seeing that Wyatt was about to take his plate to the sink, Bailey quickly rose ahead of him. Putting out her hand for his plate, she said, "I'll do that."

"Don't." It sounded more like an order than a polite admonishment to her. Bailey dropped her hand to her side. "You did the cooking," he told her without any fanfare. "I'll clean up."

It sounded more like a business deal between two strangers instead of two friends. But then, they hadn't parted as friends, she reminded herself. He probably thought it was quite the opposite.

"It's your house," she murmured, letting him have his way.

His eyes met hers. There was no softness in them. "Yes, it is."

There it was again, Bailey thought. That cold note in his voice. So cold that it could freeze an entire lake in a matter of minutes with no effort at all.

It brought back feelings of guilt to her in vivid color. She knew that there was nothing she could possibly say that would change what had happened. All she could do was try to make it up to him now by finding a way to be useful, by trying her best to find a way to get him to come around a little.

She tried talking about what she knew was dear to Wyatt's heart. "The ranch seems to be doing well," she observed. "You must be very proud."

He wasn't the type to admit things outright. "I like it," he told her evasively and then admitted, "It's a lot of work, but it's worth it."

Well, this wasn't going very well, she noted. "I saw Fox when I was leaving," she said, trying again to get some sort of conversation going between them. "Does he still live on the edge of your property?"

"Fox bought that property from me," Wyatt reminded her. "So he lives on his own place."

"Sorry, my mistake," she apologized. She'd forgotten about that. "But you still work together, right?" she asked.

Wyatt shrugged. "In a manner of speaking. He breeds horses. Some are mine," he told her.

"He always did have a way with horses." Bailey remembered. She'd missed being part of a family, even if it really wasn't her own. She thought of Fox's younger sister, who had also been adopted by Russ and Mara Colton after their parents perished in a car accident. "How's Sloane doing?"

He thought about what Fox had told him regarding his sister. "A lot better now that she's finally shed that hundred and eighty pounds that was really weighing her down."

Bailey stared at him. "What?" That didn't sound possible. She recalled Sloane being a petite, slender young woman when she'd left.

Wyatt explained his comment. "She divorced her no-good husband and, according to Fox, Sloane and Chloe will probably be moving back here soon."

"Chloe?" Bailey repeated quizzically. This was a new name for her.

"That's Sloane's two-year-old daughter," Wyatt told her.

"Sloane has a daughter?" she questioned, completely surprised at the news. It felt as if everyone was having children except for her. "I didn't even know she was married until you just said that she got a divorce."

"Yes, she did, and in her case, that's a good thing." He paused as he looked at her, his expression solemn. "I guess there's a lot of that going around."

She deserved that, Bailey thought.

"When is she thinking of coming out here?" Bailey was hoping to be able to see the woman before she had to leave.

That at least was an easy question, he thought. "Fox told me she's going to try to be here in time for Grandpa Earl's ninety-fourth birthday celebration."

"When is that?" She wanted to know.

"This weekend," he told her. Then he added a salient point. "My parents want to keep it strictly 'family only.' These days Grandpa Earl is pretty physically and mentally weak, and they don't want to tax him any more than is absolutely necessary."

That meant that she wouldn't be allowed to come, she thought. "Oh."

Wyatt heard the disappointment in her voice and told himself to ignore it. She'd made her bed.

But telling himself that didn't help. She was here and he found that he just couldn't shut her out.

"Would you want to come?" he asked her. "It's being held at the Colton Manor," he added. The Manor wasn't exactly a place that was warm and welcoming despite all its opulent décor. "You remember it, right?"

"What I remember about Colton Manor was that

you didn't really like it," she told him. "It was a beautiful place, though."

He shrugged philosophically. "Well, if you can put up with it—and my parents—you can come with me if you'd like."

She wanted to jump at the chance but she had a question for him first. She didn't want to make him any more uncomfortable than she already had.

"You don't mind your parents knowing I'm here?" Bailey asked.

"They don't exactly figure into my day-to-day life," Wyatt answered. "So, if you want to come along and wish Grandpa happy birthday, then sure—why not? Come."

She smiled widely. "Thank you," she told him. "I will."

He found that he was unable to look away. Heaven help him, though he tried to deny it, he was still a sucker for that smile.

Chapter 5

It felt strange being back here after so much time had passed, Bailey thought. It felt even stranger to be spending the night in the guest room instead of the master bedroom, beside Wyatt. But she had been the one who had left, not the other way around, so she couldn't very well expect anything else.

He'd certainly done amazing things with the house in the ensuing years, she mused. So much so that she hardly recognized it anymore. It definitely bore his own personal stamp—strong and powerful, just like the man himself. The furniture was all wood and she had a feeling that Wyatt had built it with his own hands, just as he had constructed the wrap-around porch.

The only non-masculine touch was a handful of

landscape paintings scattered throughout the ranch house that his cousin Bree had painted.

Bailey wandered over to the guest room window and looked out onto the front lawn below. That was something else that had surprised her. Wyatt had put a lot of windows in the house. It was almost as if he had made a conscious attempt to keep himself from being shut in and cut off from the rest of the world, Bailey thought.

There was a full moon out tonight and it shone on the last of the snow that stubbornly clung to the land. Since this was Colorado in January, she was confident there would be more snow before spring finally came and settled in.

Maybe even *after* spring was here, she acknowledged with a smile, recalling other springs that had had more than their share of freezing snowstorms.

Turning around, Bailey perused the guest room again. She hadn't been paying lip service earlier when she'd complimented Wyatt on what he'd done with the ranch. He'd made a real go of the place. It was a working cattle ranch just west of Roaring Springs with five hundred prime acres of grazing land and good water.

The whole place looked like a picture postcard with its impressive, beautiful mountain range visible in the distance.

All things considered, she supposed anyone would have called her a fool for leaving, but there were things that were far more important than money or having a picturesque place to live. She hadn't been her own person here; she had just been Wyatt Colton's wife. A well-meaning appendage at best. In the end, Bailey'd had the feeling that Wyatt really hadn't seen her at all anymore and the fault for that lay with her—because she wasn't anyone, not really. At best, she was just a former rodeo barrel racer who had married well. Not something that looked very compelling on a résumé, she thought ruefully.

Moreover, she and Wyatt might have started out as partners when they'd first arrived here on his grandmother's property, but as the years went on, that partnership had devolved. Instead she'd felt like she'd had a rival for Wyatt's affections, for his attention. And it wasn't even a flesh-and-blood mistress that was claiming him; it was the ranch itself.

The ranch had taken up all his time, all his focus. The part she'd played kept fading until she'd felt like just another one of the ranch hands, someone who was just there to help, nothing more. She'd had nothing of her own to point to, nothing unique to build her identity on.

So she'd made up her mind to leave and it had taken all of her courage to do that.

The first year on her own had been rocky; she'd been nursing a broken heart. Even though she'd known leaving him had been the right thing to do, she had missed him terribly. But she'd wound up making something of herself. She had graduated from veterinary school and gone on to start her own practice.

All in all, she was very proud of herself. She felt as if she finally *was* someone now.

Someone who was still lonely, Bailey thought ruefully, wandering around the darkened room. Even though she had met and interacted with a great many people as a veterinarian, at the end of the day, she was still alone.

Still not a mother.

And that ate away at her more than anything else did. She would have gladly given up everything she had managed to achieve in these last six years just to hold her own baby in her arms.

Which was why she had set aside her pride and come back here to the ranch to ask Wyatt for the ultimate favor.

A favor he still hadn't agreed to, she thought now, sitting on the bed with a sigh.

But he would, she silently promised herself. One way or another, he would. She was not going to accept failure. Not at this stage of her life.

She couldn't afford to. Despite everything that had transpired, she still loved him...

Because she hadn't packed with the idea of going to a party when she'd made up her mind to seek out her ex-husband, Bailey had nothing to wear to his grandfather's birthday party. Which was why the next day, while Wyatt was working on the ranch, Bailey drove herself into Roaring Springs' downtown area.

Downtown had changed in the last six years, as well. There were more shops and restaurants than she remembered, but then, she had never really been much of a shopper back then. The jeans and work shirts she'd favored were her attire of choice when she'd worked on the ranch. She hadn't had any need for anything fancier at the time—except when she'd finally met his family.

She discovered that most of his family hadn't cared what she'd worn to the first meeting. Happily, she'd found that his siblings and cousins had all been pretty much down-to-earth folks despite the family wealth. Moreover, she had adored his grandfather.

His parents, however, had been another story. Bailey'd found them both to be distant in different ways.

Mara Colton was an impeccable dresser. It didn't matter if she was just having breakfast with the family or attending a fund-raiser with the state's wealthiest blue bloods, Mara Colton left a huge impression. But as a mother she was a better director of operations, which was her official position at the Château. Originally a small hotel, little by little it had been transformed and was now considered to be a world-class hotel and spa that the rich and famous flocked to.

As for Wyatt's father, Russ Colton, the man was a CEO down to his very toes and far more interested in making money than in actually making a connection with members of his family.

Which essentially dashed her hopes of ever fitting

in with the Coltons. In fact, after she and Wyatt had gotten married, both his parents had made no secret of the fact that they viewed her as an interloper. And now? Well, she sincerely doubted that anything had changed for the couple in the last six years, especially since, in their estimation, she had rejected the "gift" of the Colton name and walked out on their eldest son.

However, she thought as she looked at dress after dress in the sales rack, this wasn't about her, or even about them, as intimidating as the couple was. Instead this was about Wyatt's grandfather, Earl, a lovable old man who had accepted her with open arms when she had first arrived in Roaring Springs with Wyatt.

In the end, after visiting two of the less exclusive clothing shops, Bailey wound up purchasing a tasteful navy blue dress that came down to just above her knees and accentuated her curves just enough to make her look alluring.

In a third store, Bailey managed to find just the right pair of shoes to match her dress. The heels made her taller than she already was, but she found them comfortable as well as flattering, so that sealed the deal as far as she was concerned.

With the last item selected and paid for, Bailey felt she looked good enough to remeet the family. Or at least she hoped so.

Bailey was a little less certain about that when she was sitting beside Wyatt in the car as he drove them up to the Manor later that afternoon. Butterflies multiplied and grew larger with every mile that went by.

Nestled, if that word could actually be used in describing a 35-million-dollar, 18,000-square-foot showpiece, in the mountains right above the valley, the house was unofficially referred to as Colton Manor. Painstakingly designed and decorated, the seven-bedroom, eleven-bathroom structure with its luxurious indoor pool and ornate wine cellar had all the warmth of a bitter, isolating winter blizzard.

Russ called it home, but no one else did. It had been constructed ten years ago, and by the time it was finished and ready to be inhabited, most of the Colton children had forged their own paths and made their homes somewhere else.

Bailey shifted in the passenger seat, trying not to fidget. She was anxious to have the gathering over with and yet afraid to have it over at the same time.

"Nervous?" Wyatt asked as they came closer to their destination. The massive house loomed just up ahead.

Bailey wet her lips before speaking, afraid they would stick together. "What makes you say that?"

Wyatt nodded at the fruit basket she held on her lap, a gift that at the last minute he'd decided should be from both of them.

"If you were clutching that thing any tighter, you'd wind up bringing Grandpa a basket of fruit *juice* by the time we reach the house," he commented.

Bailey loosened her fingers from around the basket. "I guess maybe I am a little nervous," she admitted. "I mean, they probably still all hate me," she added, thinking of his parents.

"If that's what you think, then why are you coming?" he wanted to know.

His question was simple enough to answer. "Because a man doesn't turn ninety-four every day and because Grandpa Earl doesn't have a single hateful bone in his body," she informed her ex-husband.

Wyatt frowned slightly, pretending to consider her words. "I don't think that's anatomically correct."

"Maybe not," Bailey allowed. "But it does accurately describe that wonderful old man."

Wyatt smiled, remembering something his grandfather had said. "He always liked you."

"The feeling was more than mutual," she was quick to assure Wyatt. "I really missed him when I left. He was like the grandfather I never had." She smiled, more to herself than at her ex-husband, but he caught a glimpse of that smile and it had its effect. "I guess the same thing could be said about your siblings," she continued. "I mean, I know I was the outsider, but they never made me feel that way," she told him.

Wyatt heard what wasn't being said. "I'm guessing the same thing couldn't have been said about my parents." Actually he didn't have to guess—he *knew*. She wouldn't have been the wife that Russ Colton would have handpicked for his oldest son. As for his mother? Well, she was far too busy running the Château to notice *anything* that didn't have to do with management. That included her son and his wife.

Bailey shrugged carelessly, avoiding Wyatt's eyes. "No, not really."

"Don't feel bad," he told her. "They didn't make me feel accepted, either," he said in all seriousness. "My parents were too busy building their careers to connect with any of the kids they'd had.

"I get the feeling that my mother regrets that now, but she had no idea how to show her affection or how to make up for the lack of it during our so-called 'formative' years. My father, on the other hand, isn't hampered by anything like that." Wyatt laughed to himself, although there was no humor evident in the sound. "The only thing Russ Colton is good at, other than earning money and envisioning himself as the head of an empire, is showing his disapproval."

Bailey knew exactly what Wyatt was referring to. She'd witnessed examples of that behavior when they had first arrived back in town and Wyatt had claimed the property that his grandmother had left him.

She felt a streak of loyalty suddenly stirring up inside her.

"He wanted you to do what he told you to," she said. "When you wouldn't, you made him angry. You always were your own person and that went against what he saw as your destiny."

"You still remember that?" Wyatt asked her, surprised.

She looked at him, wondering why he sounded so

astonished. It had only been six years, not sixty. And even then, some things left an indelible impression.

"Of course I do. Just because I didn't stay doesn't mean that my memory was wiped clean," she pointed out.

Wyatt was quiet as they drove up the long, winding road, getting closer to the Manor. He could hear Bailey drawing in a long breath as if she was bracing herself for an ordeal.

"They don't hate you," he told the woman beside him out of the blue.

She'd gotten lost in her own thoughts for a moment, giving herself a silent pep talk. She blinked, looking at Wyatt. "Excuse me?"

"You said that you thought my brothers and sisters probably all hate you. They don't. They were baffled when you left—just like I was," he couldn't help interjecting. "But they never hated you—and they don't now."

There was something about his wording that got to her. "What about you?"

It was hard putting into words just what he was feeling—and he didn't trust himself to respond.

"Why don't we just leave it at that for the time being?" Wyatt suggested.

"Fair enough."

It really wasn't, but she felt she had probably gotten off easy, so for now she left the subject alone. She had come back for one reason and that was *not* to stir the pot. Her reason first, last and foremost was to conceive a baby.

Wyatt pulled his car up in front of the house. Almost immediately a valet emerged from within the shelter of the eight-car garage. The man was bundled up in a three-quarter-length fur jacket, wool cap and leather gloves.

In Bailey's estimation he still looked as if he was cold.

The snow that had all but receded from around the Crooked C was still very much in evidence here at the Manor. Mist could be seen coming out of the valet's nose and mouth when he spoke to them.

"The others are all inside, Mr. Colton," the older gentleman said, waiting for them to get out of the car so he could properly park it.

Wyatt got out on his side.

"The rest of the family is all gathered," the valet said as he got in behind the wheel. Leaving the seat belt unbuckled, he started up the car again.

"You have valet service at the Manor now?" Bailey asked as Wyatt helped her out of the vehicle.

He offered to take the fruit basket from her, but she shook her head. Carrying it into the house was the least she could do.

They began to walk toward the house. "I think Mother borrowed him from the Château."

"Is she still managing that place?" Bailey asked, curious. "I thought she might have retired."

Wyatt took her elbow to guide her into the house

and to prevent her from falling. While much of the snow had been cleared from the walkways, there was still a little evident in spots here and there.

"To do what?" he quipped. "My father is hardly ever home. He's constantly busy doing things that she has no part in. My mother likes giving orders and being in charge. She can't do that with my father. He wouldn't allow it." Wyatt opened the door for her and held it as she walked through. He followed her in. "She needs her own kingdom to preside over. In this case, the kingdom is the Château."

They were inside now and once again the house struck her as being way too big and far too opulent to feel comfortable in. Placing the fruit basket aside on a long table that contained other offerings and gifts, Bailey began to shrug out of her coat. Suddenly she felt Wyatt's hands at her back, slipping the coat off her shoulders.

She felt a tingle down her spine but did her best to mask it. "Oh, thank you."

"Don't look so startled," Wyatt said drolly. "I still have manners."

"I never said you didn't," Bailey protested. "I just thought you'd leave me to manage on my own while you went in to join the others."

Wyatt shrugged out of his coat just as a maid came up to them. Keeping her eyes demurely down, the young woman took both their coats.

"Your mother said to tell you that everyone is

gathered in the formal living room, sir," the maid told Wyatt.

"This is why I don't come here unless I have to," Wyatt groused as he took Bailey's arm and guided her toward the room the young woman had specified.

Bailey knew she shouldn't be asking any more questions than necessary, but Wyatt had managed to arouse her curiosity. He'd been rather withdrawn, and if he was making an effort to share something, then she wasn't about to let this opportunity go. "Why?"

"I don't like being treated as if I'm better than the people my parents have working for them," he answered, keeping his voice low. "And Mother insists on it," he added just as they crossed the threshold into the huge room.

The next moment Bailey saw Wyatt's mother looking at her sharply from all the way across the room. The woman stopped talking and the rather pained smile on Bailey's face faded entirely as her former mother-in-law made eye contact with her.

Bailey squared her shoulders. She had known this wasn't going to be easy and she'd been right. But having a baby was worth any sacrifice in her estimation.

Even if it meant having to endure Mara Colton's wrath.

Without realizing it, Bailey tightened her hold on her ex-husband's arm.

Surprised, Wyatt slipped his other hand over her arm in an unspoken sign of support.

Bailey's heart pounded like a drum.

Chapter 6

Bailey quickly scanned the large room. Since the members of his family seemed to be scattered around, it took a moment for all the attendees to register.

"Looks like everyone's here," she murmured to her ex-husband.

"Almost everybody," Wyatt corrected her. "Fox hasn't gotten here yet. He said something about picking up Sloane and her daughter from the airport and bringing them back here for the celebration," he told her.

Bailey barely heard him. She'd made the mistake of looking in Mara Colton's direction again and she was now being held captive by the woman's penetrating gaze. It made her think about the story about a cobra and a mongoose.

If she had any thoughts of changing her mind at the last moment and withdrawing from the room as well as the celebration, that opportunity was now lost. Mara chose that moment to come gliding across the large room like a reigning queen deigning to acknowledge one of her lowly subjects.

Aside from the maid and a bartender, the spacious room was filled with thirteen other people, but right now those people might as well not have been there at all. The only person that Bailey was aware of at this very moment was Mara. Wyatt's mother was coming straight at her.

And then, suddenly, there was no distance between them at all.

Rather than address Bailey, Mara turned to her oldest son and looked at him with disapproval.

"Wyatt, the invitation specifically stated that the party for your grandfather was for 'family only.'" Mara cast a fleeting, dismissive glance in Bailey's direction. "You didn't say anything about bringing a last-minute guest, dear." Mara's smile was frigid and her tone was equally icy.

His mother was playing games, Wyatt thought. And he *wasn't* in the mood for any games. "This isn't a guest, Mother. This is Bailey." His voice was pleasant and even as he asked, "You remember Bailey, don't you?"

The blonde matriarch's dark blue eyes became little more than slits as she turned them toward her son's ex-wife.

"Indeed I do," Mara responded in a tone that left a great deal unsaid.

"She's not here for you, Mother," Wyatt replied in a matter-of-fact tone. "Bailey's here for Grandpa."

"Why?" Mara wanted to know. "He didn't ask for her," she retorted. Her smile grew tight.

Just then Wyatt's twin sisters, Skye and Phoebe, their hair as long and red as their mother's was short and blond, gathered around Wyatt and his former wife, their very presence interrupting what Mara was about to say in response.

Although it was obvious his sisters were surprised to see Bailey, they had come over to the trio with the intentions of defusing what could be seen, even across the room, as an extremely volatile situation in the making.

"Bailey, we didn't know you were back," Skye cried, hugging her former sister-in-law before she abruptly stopped and pulled back. She was the more outgoing, bubblier of the two, but she didn't take things for granted. "It is okay to hug you, isn't it?" she asked Bailey with a warm smile.

Bailey was extremely relieved to see a couple of friendly faces. "I'd be hurt if you didn't," she told Skye.

"Me next," Phoebe declared, opening her arms. Slightly more withdrawn than her twin, the manager of the Château was clearly still very happy, although quite surprised, to see Bailey again. She hugged Bailey as Skye stepped back.

"Speaking of 'hurt,'" Mara began crisply, unwilling to let the subject drop.

But she got no further.

"Give it a rest, Mother," Decker requested politely, joining the growing circle around his brother and the woman who had once been married to Wyatt. The manager of the Lodge smiled warmly at his former sister-in-law. "How have you been, Bailey?" he asked as he took his turn hugging her.

Mara stood back, glaring at the displays of affection and clearly annoyed that her offspring were welcoming back this outsider.

"I've been well, thank you. And busy," Bailey added, releasing Decker.

"That's *Doctor* Bailey to you," Wyatt informed his younger brother.

Heaven help him, as ticked as he was with Bailey for leaving, Wyatt had to admit that he was proud of what she had managed to accomplish.

"Doctor?" Decker repeated, by turns surprised and then impressed as he looked at Bailey. "Hey, Doc, I've got this pain right here—" he began, holding the small of his back as if talking about an actual pain rather than just teasing her.

Wyatt clipped his brother on the back of his head. "Not that kind of a doctor, you idiot. She's a vet."

"That's okay," Skye said to Wyatt. "Everyone knows that Decker behaves like an untamed animal when he loses his temper."

"Ha ha, very funny," Decker responded. And then

he looked at Bailey, curiosity entering his eyes. "A veterinarian? Really? Did you come back to Roaring Springs to practice here? Because we could certainly use a vet who lives closer to Roaring Springs than the one we've got now. The closest vet we've got actually has his practice in the next town."

Stunned, Mara looked from one of her offspring to another. "What is the matter with all of you? Have you forgotten that she just ran off without saying a single word?" Her voice was low but her tone was hard as steel. "People do not treat the Coltons that way," she insisted.

"No, we haven't forgotten about it," Decker answered, speaking up for his sisters and himself. "But if Wyatt's dealing with it, well then, so can we. Besides," he continued, flashing a warm grin at his prodigal former sister-in-law, "we've all missed her."

"Missed who?" Wyatt's uncle Calvin asked, joining the group. The shortest and thinnest of the three senior Colton brothers, as well as the most down-to-earth, Calvin looked at the cluster of people next to his brother's wife. And then recognition flashed in his eyes. "Bailey, is that you?" Recognition quickly melted into pleasure. "No one told me you were back. Audrey," he called to his wife, beckoning her over to the group, "look who's here. It's Bailey."

His declaration drew over not only his wife but his two grown children, Trey and Bree, as well.

Born nine years apart, the county sheriff and the artist were a perfect blend of both their Caucasian father and their African American mother, with creamy light brown complexions and golden-brown eyes. Although Trey acted somewhat reserved around Bailey, that was nothing unusual. Trey was and always had been a very serious, by-the-book man. Bree was also reserved but passionate about her art.

"When did you get back into town?" she asked Bailey, obviously very happy and excited to see her, much to Mara's annoyance.

Bailey noticed that everyone within the small circle was now looking at her, waiting for her answer. "Just a couple of days ago."

"She's a vet now," Skye informed her cousins proudly, as if Bailey's accomplishment was also hers.

"A vet?" Bree repeated, surprised. "You mean like a soldier?"

"No, like someone who listens to a cow with a stethoscope," Skye said with a grin before Bailey had a chance to answer Bree.

"Oh." And then Bree asked her exactly the same thing that Decker had asked. "Are you going to be opening up a practice in Roaring Springs?"

"That's still up in the air," Wyatt told his cousin, coming to Bailey's rescue. He knew that she didn't want to mention the real reason she was back and he wanted to spare them both. "She's here right now for Grandpa Earl's birthday party."

"How very lucky for us," Mara responded sarcastically then turned on her very expensive heel and walked straight to the small bar set up beside the liquor cabinet. The bartender poured her a glass of white wine before she even reached him.

"Don't mind her," Wyatt's aunt Audrey told Bailey. "She has a hard time seeing points of view that aren't her own," the philanthropist said, tongue-in-cheek. Everyone knew that Audrey was speaking from experience since Mara hadn't exactly welcomed her to the family with open arms, either.

"How long do you plan on staying if you don't open a practice?" Phoebe asked, bringing the conversation back to Bailey's sudden reappearance.

"That all depends on a lot of factors, Phoebe," Wyatt answered evasively, hoping to shut down that line of conversation.

But his sisters were nothing if not persistent. "Such as?" Skye wanted to know.

"That, little sister, is none of your business," Wyatt informed her, keeping his tone friendly but distant.

Rather than accept that, Skye turned to her former sister-in-law. "Bailey?" It was obvious she was waiting for a response from her rather than her brother.

"I honestly don't know yet," Bailey told the girl. And it was the truth. Everything was up in the air because Wyatt hadn't yet given her an answer to her initial request.

She turned to Wyatt. Bailey knew it was probably unfair, but right now she saw him as someone who would back her up. And then, changing the tone of the conversation, she told the people around her, "I haven't had a chance to pay my respects to the birthday boy yet."

"Well then, by all means, let's go correct that right now," Decker told her, taking Bailey's arm and tucking it through his.

For some reason he couldn't explain to himself, that didn't sit well with Wyatt.

"I'll handle this," he informed his brother, cutting in. Removing Bailey's arm from his brother's, Wyatt slipped her arm through his.

Bailey looked at him quizzically. She would have thought that although Wyatt was putting on a happy face for his family, she was far from his favorite person at the moment. This affectionate display struck her as being over and above the call of duty.

"Let's get you over to Grandpa before my mother finds some other reason to try to launch another attack against you," Wyatt told her in a low voice.

"I'd love to see him," Bailey replied, more than happy to talk to the old man.

The guest of honor, Earl Colton, was sitting slightly hunched over in his wheelchair. While he was still able to take a step or two on his own, the wheelchair was by far his preferred mode of getting around.

It broke Bailey's heart to see him like this. Wyatt's grandfather now looked every one of his ninety-four years and then some. His eyes were vacant as they shifted around the room.

Walking up to his grandfather, Bailey saw Wyatt transform into a smiling young man, the one she had fallen in love with so deeply despite all her promises to herself never to fall for a rodeo cowboy.

She felt her heart flutter.

"Hi, Grandpa. I brought someone to see you," Wyatt told the old man, speaking up so that Earl could hear him. "Look." He ushered Bailey forward a little so that the man could see her better. Like his hearing, Earl's vision left something to be desired. The old man could only see people and things if they were close to him.

Earl Colton, dressed up for the occasion, raised his head and looked at Bailey. He cocked his white head slightly, but his expression remained blank. There was no sign of recognition at all.

Bailey spoke up, greeting the old man. "Hello, Grandpa Earl."

Earl sat quietly in his specially fitted wheelchair, staring at her for a long moment as if attempting to place her.

Then, failing, the old man asked her, "Do I know you?"

She leaned closer to him. "Grandpa, it's me. Bailey." When her name seemed to mean nothing to him, she tried again. "I'm Bailey Norton." Still nothing, so she said, "Wyatt's wife."

Funny how right that sounded even though it was no longer true, she couldn't help thinking.

Bailey slanted a look at Wyatt to see if referring to herself as his wife bothered him or had unearthed any hurt feelings.

But Wyatt seemed totally unaffected by her reference to herself. Instead he was focused on his grandfather's condition, which really concerned him.

"He's been getting slowly worse," he confided to

Bailey, lowering his voice. Earl didn't seem to hear him at all. "He doesn't have Alzheimer's," Wyatt told her, "but his memory winks in and out a great deal, and these last few months, Grandpa doesn't seem to recognize people very much anymore," he added sadly. "We wanted to make this a really good party because…well…"

Wyatt's voice trailed off. He couldn't bring himself to say any of the harsh words that had been plaguing his mind of late. Saying them out loud didn't improve the situation in any way and it didn't change it, either. It just underscored it.

It was what it was, Wyatt thought philosophically. But he'd be damned if he didn't do his best to make this birthday party as memorable as it could be for the senior Colton.

Meanwhile, Bailey had bent even lower to get as close to the old man as she could. Looking him directly in the eye, she took Earl's hand in hers and smiled at him.

"I hope you have a really wonderful birthday today, Grandpa. And I'm very glad to be here to share it with you."

Earl's eyes met hers and there was still no sign of any recognition in them. But she could have sworn she felt him squeeze her hand ever so slightly. It told her that somewhere within him, the soul of the man she had once known still existed.

She squeezed his hand back.

Just then the sound of a door being closed echoed in the background. Mara frowned, her annoyance clearly spiking. And then the sound of small feet pounding on the family matriarch's expensive marble floors was heard growing closer.

Mara appeared ready to dispatch the maid to silence whatever was going on, but she never got the chance because a moment later Fox walked in, his sister, Sloane, right beside him.

"We made it!" Fox declared triumphantly to his cousins. "We came straight from the airport." He beamed at his sister and his little niece. "They didn't want to miss a minute of Grandpa's party."

"Fox, I *can* talk for myself, you know," Sloane Colton Durant, a petite, dark-haired attorney, told her older brother. Her eyes passed over Bailey and then went straight to Wyatt. She looked at him quizzically, as if silently asking if she could acknowledge his ex-wife or if she was supposed to just pretend the other woman wasn't there.

Wyatt nodded imperceptibly just before he hugged his cousin. "It's really great to see you smiling again, Sloane." Releasing her, he took a step back. "How are you doing?"

"Better now that I'm with family," Sloane told him honestly. There were emotional wounds, but they would heal. She just needed time.

Sloane raised her brow slightly, still rather uncertain how her cousin felt about having his ex-wife here.

"It's okay," Wyatt told her quietly, leaving it up to Sloane to read whatever she wanted into his statement.

Sloane took it from there. Relieved, she turned to

Bailey and smiled. "Long time no see," she said by way of a greeting.

"Yes, you might say that," Bailey responded then laughed as she hugged the other woman.

And as she hugged Sloane, she felt something that only came up to her waist wiggling in between her and the other, younger woman, as if unwilling to be left out. Bailey looked down and saw a miniature version of Sloane smiling up at her. She felt a sudden pang and managed to smile her way through it.

"Hi," she said, greeting the small person. "What's your name?"

"Chlo-wee," the little girl responded, pushing her thumb against her small chest to indicate that was her. Her eyes were sparkling with a very pleased look, as if she was happy to be able to answer the question for herself.

"Well, Chloe," Bailey told Sloane's daughter, "you're adorable."

The little girl solemnly nodded. "I know," she answered as if being adorable was a given she was well aware of.

"I'm sorry," Sloane laughed, ruffling her daughter's blond hair. "I'm afraid she hasn't learned how to be modest yet."

"She has more than enough time for that," Bailey assured Wyatt's adopted sister. "Meanwhile, she *is* adorable."

Suddenly they heard Earl actually chuckling. When they turned toward the old man, they saw that Chloe had darted over to her great-grandfather. The little girl was dancing in front of him, gleefully wiggling her little hips like a hula dancer in training.

Grandpa Earl was clearly delighted by the performance.

Chapter 7

"Looks like your little girl is a miracle worker," Whit Colton observed as he came up to his niece and nephew.

At sixty years of age, Whit Colton was the youngest of the three senior Colton brothers, as well as the most concerned with his appearance. He was also considered to be the family's international playboy. He maintained a home in France as well as one in New York. Good-looking and self-assured as well as incredibly charming, Whit had never been married. It took only a few minutes in the man's company to see that Whit apparently enjoyed and thrived on his present way of life.

Whit's son, Remy, director of PR for the Empire, was also present. The Colton playboy had once had a fling with model Cordelia Ripley, which had produced a child that Cordelia had dumped on the Coltons at age five. Remy's Colton grandparents adored him, but his younger half brother, Cordelia's son by another relationship, hadn't fared so well. Seth Harris had had a rough start in life, but the Coltons had welcomed him into their fold, including to this party.

Sloane and Fox now turned to their uncle in response to his comment and Whit pointed to his father. Instead of sitting in his wheelchair with the same vacant look on his face, Earl Colton was not only laughing as he watched his great-granddaughter dancing in front of his chair, the old man was suddenly doing something he used to do when all his grandchildren were very young.

He began to wiggle his extremely bushy eyebrows. The tufted gray-and-white brows looked like two caterpillars involved in a mating ritual.

Mesmerized, Chloe abruptly stopped dancing and just stared at the unusual sight. Covering her mouth, the little girl started laughing as she saw her great-grandfather move his eyebrows at first independently of each other and then moving them in concert as if in time to some unheard music in his head.

Delighted, Chloe clapped her hands together and cried, "Again! Do it again G-Papa!"

"'G-Papa'?" Wyatt repeated. He looked at Chloe's mother for an explanation of this new term.

Sloane laughed. "Chloe can't get her tongue around

'Great-Grandpa,' so I thought this might be easier for her," she explained.

"It's perfect," Bailey told Sloane, totally delighted by the little girl. She was also thrilled to see Wyatt's grandfather behaving the way he had before his mind had begun to wander away from him.

Perfect.

The word echoed in Wyatt's head, almost mocking him. He had just glanced in Bailey's direction and seen that smile on her face, that perfect, guileless smile that had always been his undoing. He struggled mightily against falling into the trap that having her here like this created for him.

With absolutely no effort at all, he could see himself setting aside the barriers he had erected. Moreover, he could actually see himself slipping back into the life he had thought they were going to share together. The life he had forced himself to go on creating after Bailey had left him.

It was all here, ready for her.

Ongoing.

All it needed was for her to just walk right back into it.

Who was he kidding? Wyatt silently upbraided himself.

It wasn't going to be that easy. Even if Bailey *did* decide to stay, which she hadn't even hinted that she was considering, he would always be mentally looking over his shoulder, waiting for her to take off again for another unknown reason. And this time possibly taking their child with her if the scenario Bailey had painted was carried out.

No, he was better off when he adhered to the rule he had set down for himself when she had left him. *Keep your heart under lock and key. Trust no one. That way you can't be hurt.*

It was a sound rule, Wyatt thought, even though it was a lonely one.

"Hey, Wyatt, come out, come out, wherever you are," Fox was saying to him, leaning in and getting right into his face.

Rousing himself, Wyatt blinked as he looked at his brother. "What?"

"Where are you, man? Our mother just announced that we're all supposed to go to the formal dining room for dinner and to have some of Grandpa Earl's birthday cake." An easygoing smile graced Fox's lips. "I figure you could be our guide. Otherwise, Sloane and I'll probably get lost. I still can't get used to this place," he confessed, adding, "This is the biggest damn house I've ever seen."

"Well, it's not like you haven't been here before," Wyatt pointed out even as he began to lead the way to the dining room.

"Not often enough to know my way around." Fox glanced around as they were walking. "No offense," he murmured, keeping his voice low, "but who the hell needs this much space?"

"Apparently our father, who feels this house is rather small," Wyatt said as he turned a corner. He noticed that Bailey, Sloane and Fox all made sure to turn with him. Chloe was ahead of them, sitting on Earl's lap and giggling as Whit pushed his father into the dining room.

"Yeah, maybe it is—*for a castle*," Fox interjected with a touch of sarcasm.

Bailey wholeheartedly agreed with Wyatt's brother, but she kept her thoughts to herself. She didn't want to risk saying anything that would put her possibly even further on Mara's bad side than she probably already was.

She knew that Wyatt didn't need his parents' approval and most likely didn't care about their opinion one way or another, but the fact remained that she knew he *did* love his parents. Having her create any sort of waves, even very small ones, wouldn't exactly cull any favors.

When in doubt, Bailey thought, it was best to say nothing. So she kept silent.

Earl's birthday celebration lasted a total of three hours. Although gifts were brought, the old man took no notice of them and didn't react when Russ opened the gifts for him, placing them around his father.

The only "thing" the ninety-four-year-old seemed to respond to and care about was the little two-year-old girl who had remained seated on his lap through most of the celebration.

Chloe made the old man laugh and Earl in turn made her do the same. Bailey noticed that Wyatt's grandfather actually looked really pleased when he heard the light, happy sound coming from Chloe. She thought it very sweet that the two managed to bond the way they did.

But by and by, the old man dozed off in his chair, tired out by the festivities and by having so many people around him.

Edwin, the medically licensed caregiver retained by the family, who for the last five years had looked after Earl's needs, attending to the man around the clock five days a week, took one look at Earl and nodded. "Looks like you're all tuckered out, Mr. Colton," Edwin said to the old man, talking to Earl as if he was talking to a very young child. "It's time to get you into bed."

Moving to the back of the wheelchair, Edwin released the chair's two brakes and began to push it toward the hallway.

The gentle movement suddenly woke Earl.

Earl blinked the sleep out of his eyes and looked around, then looked back over his shoulder, trying to see who was pushing his wheelchair.

"Eddie?" he asked uncertainly.

Edwin peered around the man's shoulder so Earl could see him. "Right here, Mr. Colton. It's time for you to get to bed," the caregiver reiterated to the old man.

"Already?" Earl asked, the corners of his mouth drooping in disappointment.

"I'm afraid so. It's been a very long day for you," Edwin told him.

In response, Earl yawned. "Yes, it has," the old man mumbled, addressing the admission to himself. And then his head drooped a little, as if to punctuate his words.

Wyatt's grandfather was asleep before his caregiver could wheel him out of the room.

"Guess that's our cue to leave," Wyatt said to Bailey. He made no attempt to hide the fact that he was relieved his obligation was over.

All around them, family members were preparing to depart, as well.

Bailey glanced over to where Sloane had been standing. The latter had picked her daughter up in her arms and was carrying her out of the room. Bailey looked on enviously as she watched the little girl lean her head against Sloane's shoulder. Chloe's eyes were shut and her breathing was even.

It looked like heaven to Bailey.

"Looks like Grandpa wasn't the only one who fell asleep," she commented in a soft voice, careful not to wake Chloe.

Making a decision, Bailey wove her way over to Wyatt's cousin.

"May I?" she asked, nodding at the sleeping girl in Sloane's arms.

Sloane made no response for a moment and Bailey was afraid she'd presumed too much. But then Sloane said, "Sure."

Very carefully, she transferred her sleeping child into Bailey's open arms. Once she had Chloe, Bailey slowly closed her arms around the sleeping child. All sorts of emotions raced through her as she pressed the little girl closer to her, absorbing the way Chloe's heart felt beating against hers.

This was what it would be like having a child of her own, Bailey thought, the yearning within her increasing tenfold. Inhaling deeply, Bailey could have sworn that Chloe still had the new baby smell about her, even though she knew that, logically, it wasn't possible. Chloe was two years old, not two months.

Even so, it felt heavenly holding her like this.

Bailey closed her eyes and pretended, just for the space of a fleeting moment, that Chloe was *her* little girl.

Hers and Wyatt's.

With her whole heart and soul, she fervently wished it was so.

"Give Sloane back her daughter," Wyatt whispered to his ex-wife, his voice causing everything she'd been feeling right at this moment to break apart and dissolve. "She has to get going and so do we," he added matter-of-factly.

Mentally shrugging off all the emotions she'd been experiencing, Bailey forced herself to come to.

"Of course," she responded a little too quickly. She handed the sleeping little girl back to Sloane. "Thank you," Bailey told the other woman.

"No problem," Sloane assured her, a warm smile on her lips. "You looked good, holding Chloe. You ever consider having one of your own?" she asked Bailey.

The question felt like a knife cutting right into her heart.

Only every moment of every day, Bailey answered Wyatt's sister silently. Out loud she kept her response vague, saying only, "Maybe someday."

She was certain she sensed Wyatt looking at her, but when she turned her head, her ex-husband was looking straight ahead as he guided her toward the Manor's tall, imposing front doors.

Blinking back tears, Bailey felt it best to just remain silent.

Mara was there in the foyer, apparently waiting to send them all off on their way. All except for Whit, who had gone in the opposite direction, making his way deep into the Manor's interior. Whenever he was in Colorado, Whit always stayed at the Manor.

"Thank you all for coming," Mara said, addressing her children as well as the attending nephews and nieces en masse. "It meant a lot to your grandfather to have you all go out of your way to be here," she told them.

Mara sounded rather uncomfortable and stiff as she spoke. This was obviously an ordeal for her, but she was old school and that meant she felt certain amenities were required of her as the family matriarch.

"Except for when Chloe got Grandpa to laugh

with that little dance of hers, I'm not so sure he even knew we were there," Trey told his aunt.

Mara looked a little miffed as well as ruffled to have Trey contradict her. The semblance of the smile she'd been wearing faded from her perfectly made-up lips.

"He knew," Mara informed her nephew. There was no arguing with her tone.

Wyatt was relieved when Trey chose not to dispute Mara's statement further. There was clearly nothing to be gained and a possible argument in the offing if his cousin challenged what she'd said.

"Maybe he did at that," Trey agreed with a careless shrug.

As if by unspoken agreement, the attending family members left the Manor slowly. This allowed the two valets brought in just for the occasion to fetch each of the guests' cars in a less than frantic fashion. No one missed the fact that it was all conducted beneath Mara's watchful eye.

"Does your mother ever relax?" Bailey asked Wyatt when they finally got into his vehicle and began to drive away from the snow-covered Manor. She felt as if she could finally relax herself. It had felt as if Mara had been watching her the entire time.

"Not that I've ever seen," Wyatt admitted. He kept his eyes on the road as he spoke. "It's like if she ever lets her guard down, one of her hairs might suddenly *not* be in place. Looking perfect and making sure everything is running flawlessly is all that really seems to matter to my mother."

"Too bad she doesn't put the same sort of value on being a mother," Bailey commented more to herself than to Wyatt. She wasn't really sure just how he would respond to hearing criticism of his mother coming from someone else—especially her.

Wyatt shrugged. "It wasn't what she wanted to do," he told her. "Although, like I said, I get the feeling that at this stage of her life, she's harboring some vague regrets that maybe she shouldn't have dropped the ball and let a squadron of nannies and doting grandparents wind up raising all of her offspring."

Bailey shook her head. "You make the whole process sound so antiseptic."

"For her, it was," Wyatt answered.

For several minutes there was silence in the car and then Wyatt spoke up again, making an observation. "Well, you look like you managed to survive the celebration pretty well tonight."

She did, didn't she? Bailey thought, pleased with how *most* of the party had gone. She had been worried for no reason.

"That's because they didn't turn out to be angry with me the way I was afraid they'd be," she confessed.

"They're my brothers and sisters and cousins," he pointed out. "Not a pack of wild wolves."

"I know," Bailey allowed, "but I didn't know really what to anticipate—except when it came to your mother, of course. I knew she'd be angry that I showed up."

He laughed dryly. Bailey wasn't seeing the picture the way it was. "Mother was angry because she felt you insulted the Colton name, not because she thought you hurt me. Even when she brought that point up," he remembered, "it was just to stick it to you for the insult you had committed, not because she was angry on my behalf. I don't think she could even conceive of one person hurting another in that way."

There was something in his voice that had her looking at him more closely—and feeling terrible about what he had gone through. "I'm really sorry that you were hurt because of what I did, Wyatt. And I'm also sorry that your mother wasn't incensed for you. You deserved better," she told him sincerely.

"What?" He wanted to know. "A better mother or a better—?"

Bailey didn't wait for him to finish the question. "Both," she answered quickly, not wanting him to say the words.

She had a feeling that hearing him say it would hurt her far more than it would him. She had the impression that he had gotten over her a long time ago. Which was why she was really surprised he'd said he was thinking over her request and even more surprised that he had actually taken her to the family celebration.

It occurred to her that she hadn't really told him she was grateful. "Thank you for taking me to Grandpa Earl's party."

Wyatt shrugged. He didn't want her making a

big deal out of it, especially now that it was behind them. "There was room in the car," he said in a disinterested voice.

Bailey shook her head. "Don't do that," she told him softly.

He spared her a quick glance. "Do what?"

"Shrug it off when someone wants to thank you for doing something nice," she told him. "When *I* thank you for doing something thoughtful."

He fell silent again and she thought that the rest of the trip was going to be spent that way, in oppressive silence. But then he turned his head to her unexpectedly and said, "I made up my mind about your request."

Everything inside her stiffened and she waited for the inevitable words she was dreading. He was going to say no. She might as well not prolong this, she told herself miserably.

"And what did you decide?" Bailey asked, the words all but sticking to the roof of her mouth before she managed to get them out.

"Yes."

Chapter 8

Bailey's heart leaped with joy. She pressed her lips together, afraid she was jumping to conclusions. She turned to look at Wyatt just as they approached the ranch house.

Their house. Or at least it had been once.

He'd said yes.

But maybe what he was ultimately referring to was something else in their conversation, not the subject that had been so near and dear to her heart these last few weeks while she had wrestled with what to do.

"Excuse me?" Bailey asked in a barely audible voice.

Wyatt kept his eyes on the road. They were almost there. "I said yes."

Her breath caught in her throat, suspended. "To—?"

This time he spared another glance in her direction. "I don't remember seeing you drink anything tonight."

"I didn't," she protested, "other than that lemonade that was being served."

Say the words, Wyatt. Tell me what I want to hear so that there's no mistake. Please.

He pulled his vehicle into the garage next to the ranch house and she heard him exhale in muted exasperation.

"Well, you're way too young for dementia. So why are you having trouble understanding what it is that I'm telling you?"

Bailey got out of the vehicle, attempting to collect her thoughts before answering him.

"Maybe because this is something I've been thinking about and hoping for, for a very long time, and hearing you agree to it somehow just doesn't seem quite real to me yet," she told him honestly. "At the risk of having you change your mind, what just made you say yes?"

Closing the door, he walked out of the garage and toward the house.

Wyatt shrugged in response to her question. "I watched you with Sloane's daughter just before we left. Holding her, you looked as if you'd just died and gone to heaven. Doesn't seem fair to me for you to spend a lifetime deprived of having your own child if you can feel that way about someone else's. Since, according to you, time seems to be a factor, I guess I'm elected," he told her.

Bailey's eyes filled with tears. "Thank you," she whispered, doing her best not to choke up or cry.

Wyatt chuckled and she could see that he was somewhat embarrassed at the turn the conversation had taken.

"Not exactly the kind of thing I've ever been thanked for before," he said, opening the front door. He held it open for Bailey before walking in himself.

"I guess this *is* a rather unusual situation," Bailey agreed. Even as she spoke, she could feel her cheeks growing red.

She looked so vulnerable right now, he thought.

With effort, Wyatt held himself in check. The last thing either one of them needed was for this to take a wrong turn. She wasn't there because she missed him or because she felt she'd acted rashly. Her reason for being there was simply practical and he couldn't allow himself to get carried away.

He cleared his throat, as if to wipe away his thoughts. "Listen, it's getting late and I need to get an early start in the morning…"

"Anything I can do to help?" Bailey offered.

The way he'd felt when he'd walked in that evening six years ago to find her gone came rushing back to him. He felt himself stiffening.

"I thought your whole point was to get away from ranching," he reminded her coldly.

"No, that wasn't the point at all." It was late and

she wasn't up to getting into it just now with him. He had just agreed to help her with her fondest wish. She couldn't risk alienating him, especially now.

"Oh?"

The way he said the single word told her that he wasn't about to believe her denial. She had to stop talking, Bailey thought. She didn't want to say anything that would set him off.

"Like I said," Wyatt went on, "it's getting late. Why don't we pick this up tomorrow?"

She was right. Wyatt was being aloof again. Removed. That moment they had briefly shared was gone.

"Sure," she agreed. "Whatever works for you is fine with me."

Having said that, she walked through the ranch house just ahead of him and went straight to the room she was staying in. Frustration and anger accompanied her. Closing the door, she flipped the lock. Hard.

She told herself not to cry.

She didn't listen.

Bailey didn't get much sleep that night.

She was up early the next morning, before first light. But Wyatt had gotten up ahead of her. He was already dressed and in the kitchen, making short work of the extra-large mug of coffee in his hands.

He'd never been able to do a day's work without a substantial breakfast, Bailey thought. He couldn't have changed that much.

"You haven't had breakfast, have you?" she asked him, glancing at the sink. There were no dishes, no frying pan, nothing to indicate he'd had anything to eat this morning.

In response, Wyatt raised his mug, as if to show her that was enough to hold him. He took another long sip, allowing the hot black liquid to warm him.

She shook her head. That wasn't enough to sustain him.

"Give me a few minutes and I'll make you breakfast," she told him.

He frowned, setting the mug down. "You don't have to."

"I didn't say anything about 'have to,'" Bailey pointed out cheerfully.

Opening the refrigerator, she took out enough eggs for both of them, along with bread and butter. She found a couple of slices of ham pushed over to the back on the bottom shelf. In her estimation, they had to be used soon or thrown out.

"I don't have time to wait for all this," Wyatt informed her curtly.

He'd agreed to do what she'd wanted, but that didn't mean he wanted them growing close.

"You're the boss, aren't you?" Bailey asked, moving around quickly. "You can show up a few minutes late. The ranch and the cattle'll still be there. Besides, I happen to know that you're a lot nicer on a full stomach than an empty one. Think of it as doing it for your men," she encouraged.

She continued moving around quickly as she got breakfast ready, bringing to mind a general whipping troops into shape.

He knew that mode, remembered it from their time together. There was no stopping her. He might as well not fight it and just eat breakfast.

"I guess I can spare a few minutes," Wyatt allowed grudgingly.

She glanced at him over her shoulder. "Thank you."

"You're patronizing me," he accused.

Finished, she turned around. "I wouldn't dream of it," she answered innocently.

"There," she declared triumphantly, sliding the impromptu omelet she'd made onto his plate. She cut a small piece of the omelet for herself, putting it onto another plate. "If you remember to chew and not wolf it down, you still shouldn't lose too much time getting out there," she told him.

He shook his head as he took his seat. "You're still bossy, aren't you?"

"I'll have you know I was *never* bossy," she contradicted. "I just knew better."

Wyatt laughed dryly but the corners of his mouth curved. For now, he didn't bother disputing Bailey's statement.

Taking a sip of his coffee, she made a face as she set his mug down.

"Your coffee still tastes like tar," she told him. She'd taken the sip for warmth and deeply regretted it.

"I like it that way."

"You have to say that," she replied. When he raised his eyebrow, she explained. "It's not in you to admit I'm right."

He just gave her a dark look then quickly finished the rest of his omelet.

He was done and grabbing his hat less than five minutes after she had set the plate in front of him.

The front door opened just as he was reaching for his jacket. Hank Wilson, one of his ranch hands, hurried in. By the agitated look on the young hand's face, it was obvious that something was wrong.

"You're going to want to come quick, boss," Hank told him.

Instantly alert as he shrugged into his jacket, Wyatt asked, "Why? What's the matter?"

"Something's wrong with Annabelle," Hank said, all but tripping over his tongue. "This isn't going like the last one did. I don't think the calf's coming out right," Hank told him. "I think she needs help," he added nervously.

"Make sense, Hank. What are you talking about?" Wyatt demanded as he hurried toward the front door.

Bailey was immediately on her feet. "Is it her time?" When the hand turned to look at her blankly, she restated the question. "Is Annabelle giving birth?"

Wyatt didn't answer her. He pushed Hank out the door ahead of him and quickly followed, his mind on saving his milk cow.

Biting off an exasperated curse, Bailey rushed

after him, barely stopping to grab her own jacket from the coat tree next to the front door.

Never breaking stride, she hurried into the jacket. "Wyatt, wait up!" she called after her ex-husband. She paused only long enough to pull out the black bag that she'd stashed in the closet.

"I don't have time to answer your questions," Wyatt snapped, not even bothering to look over his shoulder.

"I'm a vet, Wyatt, remember?" she all but shouted at his back. "I might be able to help."

There was no "might" about it. She was confident that she really *could* help, but now wasn't the time to sound as if she was bragging. There was no time to get into an argument if the milk cow was in trouble, which, judging from the ranch hand's tone, she was.

"I've got my medical bag right here," she told Wyatt, holding the bag aloft so he could see it if he bothered to turn around.

He did and then looked surprised. "You brought your bag?" he questioned.

"Absolutely," she answered, catching up to him. "I spent a lot of time getting that degree. I'm not about to leave the tools of my trade behind."

Just for a moment, Bailey thought she saw something in Wyatt's eyes.

Admiration? Respect?

Before she could pin it down, the look was gone.

Maybe it was just wishful thinking on her part, she thought.

The main barn wasn't located all that far from the ranch house. The moment they walked in, Bailey could see that the milk cow was in trouble. Pacing, Annabelle lay down in the stall, first on her knees, then completely down. The pregnant milk cow definitely looked to be distressed.

Tossing off her jacket, Bailey sank beside the animal. Annabelle became more agitated. Bailey began to speak to the cow in a low, soothing voice.

Afraid, and clearly in pain, the milk cow pulled away, making a mournful noise. Bailey persisted, talking to Annabelle and trying to get her to calm down.

"What's the matter, honey? That little girl inside you doesn't want to come out?"

Opening her bag, she took out a large, long pair of gloves and pulled them on. The gloves went all the way up and over her biceps. She had no idea how far up she was going to need to go.

"Okay, girl, let's just see what the problem is," Bailey told her.

With slow, deliberate movements so as not to frighten the animal or cause the milk cow to pull back, Bailey put her hands all the way inside the pregnant cow. She felt slowly around.

"That's what I thought," Bailey said more to herself than to the man hovering over her.

"What is it? What's wrong with her?" Wyatt demanded.

Bailey glanced up at him. "The calf's breech."

"Lots of calves are born breech," he said in response. "But I'm guessing that this isn't just the run-of-the-mill kind of breech, is it?"

Bailey shook her head. "It feels like the head is coming first, not the feet."

This wasn't good. "Am I going to lose her?" Wyatt braced for the worst.

"Not if I can help it," Bailey told him with determination. "I want you to pet her and talk to her. She knows your voice better than mine," she said before turning to the ranch hand who looked more like a worried father than a cowboy. "Hank, get me a basin of hot water and some towels."

Wilson was gone before she could even finish her sentence.

"What are you planning on doing?" Wyatt asked her, dropping to his knees beside the milk cow as he started doing what Bailey had told him to do.

"I'm going to do my best to turn that calf so it can come out without causing any damage to his mother or to himself."

Wyatt looked at her skeptically. This was a whole new side to Bailey and he wasn't sure if he was buying into it.

"You ever do that before?" he queried.

Bailey avoided his eyes. "Don't ask questions you don't want to hear the answer to," she replied.

"Then you *haven't* done this before," he concluded, far from reassured. "Look, I can call Doc Elroy from the next town. He can be out here in—"

"Not enough time," she said, cutting him off. "And

to answer your question, I've observed it being done. Don't worry," she told him. "I can do this. Now let's get this done. We don't have much time." Bailey looked at the milk cow. Annabelle was really in pain and it would only get worse if they didn't act fast. "This is going to hurt me more than you, Annabelle."

"I'm betting not in the same place it isn't," Wyatt murmured, momentarily lightening the mood.

Bailey glanced in his direction just as Hank stumbled back in with the basin of water and the towels she'd sent him to get.

"Just reassure her," she told Wyatt.

She put her hands back inside the animal. There were a variety of breech positions the calf could be in and righting a calf was not such an easy matter.

Bailey did it by very slow increments, doing her best not to hurt the cow or the calf and not to frighten Annabelle. To accomplish what she was trying to do, she needed the milk cow to be kept perfectly still.

Wyatt and Hank managed to hold Annabelle relatively still for the duration of the process.

It felt to Bailey as if time had stopped. It was marked only by the sound of the cow's labored breathing and the feel of perspiration trickling down the small of her own back.

Bailey could feel her heart pounding as well as the cow's heart and that of her as yet unborn calf. At one point it felt as if all three were in harmony.

Holding her breath, Bailey pushed the calf back into the uterus then grasped the upper leg and pushed it just enough to bring the knee forward. With the calf's knee lightly flexed, she cupped the hood with her hand and then gently but firmly brought the leg up to a normal position.

"C'mon, honey, just a little more. You can do this." And suddenly, after what seemed like an eternity, she finally had all four of the calf's legs in the right positions.

"Showtime, darlin'," Bailey told the calf's mother. "Let's see that pretty little face. Oh! Here she comes," she cried, relieved and delighted at the first sign of the placental sac emerging. "Just a little more and then you can rest easy. C'mon, you can do this, Annabelle. You can do this!"

Bailey caught herself praying, mentally reciting prayers from her childhood, prayers she hadn't even thought she even remembered. But she did.

And then she was finally rewarded with the low sound of mooing. Annabelle's brand-new calf had come into the world.

Bailey wasn't sure if it was perspiration or tears she felt on her cheeks. She was far too exhausted to care. She felt as if she'd run three marathons in the space of time it had taken to bring this new life, healthy and strong, into the world.

"Looks like you have a daughter, not a son, Annabelle," she told the milk cow.

Annabelle turned her head to the new life that had just joined them, licking her baby and cleaning her up.

"It's alive," Wyatt cried in wonder and relief.

Bailey blew out a breath. "Certainly looks that way, doesn't it?" she asked. Exhausted, she felt wobbly herself as she stood. She brushed the perspiration away from her forehead with the back of her arm. She couldn't remember when she had felt such a sense of satisfaction and accomplishment.

She couldn't stop smiling.

"You did good, Bailey," Wyatt told her gruffly.

Now that it was over, she could breathe again. "Annabelle did all the work. I was just there, overseeing the project," she said.

The next moment she felt like collapsing into a grateful heap right next to the cow. She managed to keep herself upright, although it wasn't easy.

And then she felt Wyatt's arms, coming from behind and slipping around her shoulders. She felt him hug her in gratitude.

"You did good," he repeated, this time with more feeling. He wasn't about to let her just shrug off what she had accomplished. "Annabelle could have died without you. Her calf, too." He had seen it happen more than once.

"Luckily, we'll never know," Bailey told him. She sagged against his hard chest for a second, trying to pull herself together. Then, blowing out a long breath, she rallied and turned her head to him. "Well, now that mother and baby seem to be doing well, I'd better get back and do those dishes we left in the sink," she told him.

"The dishes can wait a little longer," Wyatt informed her.

"Okay," she agreed. "Is there anything else you want me to help with?"

Instead of answering her, Wyatt turned her to face him.

And then he kissed her.

Chapter 9

The kiss caught her completely by surprise. As did her own reaction to it.

Time suddenly stood still.

Bailey had always known that she had never stopped loving Wyatt even after she'd left him. Even after she had sent him the signed divorce papers that signaled the end of their marriage.

But the intensity of her response to his kiss took her totally, utterly, by surprise.

It was as if a squadron of rockets had just taken off, lighting up a heretofore entirely darkened sky.

She was aware of *everything*, even the most minute action. Aware that Wyatt had taken her face in his hands, cupping it gently the way she'd always loved, just before kissing her. Aware of the way his lips felt touching hers.

Aware of the sultry, seductive taste of him and how her head was spinning like a top that had gone completely out of control.

And oh so aware that his kiss had her blood rushing through her veins like molten lava about to come shooting out of a volcano.

Falling deeper into the kiss, Bailey caught hold of his big, strong arms, desperate to anchor herself. Otherwise she was certain she would wind up sinking bonelessly onto the ground, embarrassing herself in front of Wyatt and his ranch hands.

She knew he wouldn't appreciate that.

At the last available moment, Bailey kissed him back. Kissed him with a verve that had been missing from her life for more than six years because near the end, they had become just two strangers living in the same unfinished house.

Taking a breath to steady herself, afraid that what was happening between them was on the verge of getting out of hand, Bailey forced herself to pull back. She raised her eyes to Wyatt's, looking for some sort of explanation for what had just transpired.

Kissing her had been a momentary, impetuous act on his part, done without any thought. He'd just gone with his gut—and he was now paying the consequences. Because kissing Bailey had brought back a flood of emotions he could have sworn he'd managed to bury so deep, there was no way to ever resurrect them.

He had been wrong.

Taking a breath, trying to clear his head and to find some way to explain what had just happened, Wyatt murmured, "I guess you really are a veterinarian, aren't you?"

"That's what it says on my diploma," Bailey responded, trying to sound glib.

She had no idea that Wyatt could shake her up like this. She felt like a giddy teenager, except that she was neither of those things.

Bailey glanced around to see if others had been watching. Mercifully, the ranch hands had had the decency to pretend their attention was elsewhere.

"You sure I can't help out here?" she asked him. The idea of going back to the house, to be alone with her thoughts and all the feelings that Wyatt had managed to unearth, was definitely not appealing to her right now. She both needed and wanted to keep busy.

Wilson suddenly looked up, coming to her rescue. "Boss, Peters is still in his bunk with that case of food poisoning, so we are shorthanded," the ranch hand told Wyatt. "We could use another set of hands."

Bailey immediately jumped at the chance. "See, I could help," she told Wyatt, nodding her head in Wilson's direction.

Wyatt looked at his ex skeptically. "You sure you want to do this?"

Bailey was enthusiastic about the idea of remaining out on the range, working alongside the rest of the ranch hands.

"I never minded the work," she reminded him, even when there were just the two of them. In some ways, doing that back then had made them closer— until making the ranch a success was all there was.

Wyatt was silent for a moment. He wasn't sure if he wanted her around, at least not where he could easily see her whenever he looked up. The kiss had been his fault, but the feelings that Bailey had aroused were way too fresh, all too close to the surface, right now for him to be able to deal with them properly.

But he knew that his hands were all looking at him. Having Bailey help out today was the logical thing to agree to. If he didn't, he felt the men would know why and that might wind up diminishing him in their eyes. He had no choice but to agree.

"Sure—why not?" Wyatt said with a careless shrug. "We need to check on the rest of the herd," he told her. "Make sure they haven't wandered off while we were focused on Annabelle."

Relieved, she smiled. "Just point me in the right direction."

The direction he really wanted to point her in was toward the ranch house. Or, better yet, back to wherever it was that she'd come from before showing up on his doorstep, but he knew that he wasn't free to do either one.

So instead Wyatt told her, "You're coming with me," and started to lead the way to the stables.

Bailey picked up speed so she wouldn't wind up falling behind. And then she realized where they were going.

"We're riding?"

He nodded. "Still the best way to herd cattle considering some of this terrain." And then it occurred to him that she might not be entirely comfortable with what he was suggesting. "When was the last time you were on a horse?"

Bailey waved aside his concerns. "Don't worry about me. I grew up in a saddle, remember? It's not something I'd forget how to do just because I've taken a little break from riding."

"How little?"

"Never mind. I can still outride you," Bailey informed him, dismissing his question.

Bailey wasn't given to bragging, he knew that. If she was confident, it was for a reason. He needed to get his mind back on the ranch.

"Then let's get to it," he told her, going to get his saddle.

"I'm not sure about the exact number, but I'm pretty sure that every bone in my body is aching," Bailey commented some eight hours later when they'd finally called it a day and had wrapped things up.

They were both in the stable, unsaddling their horses. "And if my head was any heavier, I don't think I could hold it up," she added.

Wyatt hung up his horse's bridle. "Now you're just

exaggerating," he laughed, removing the mount's blanket.

"No, I'm not," Bailey countered. She hated to admit it, but she could barely lift her arms. She was beyond exhausted. "I guess I am out of practice," she admitted, pulling the saddle off the horse she'd ridden for the better part of the day.

"You looked as if you were doing fine to me," he told her.

"Thanks," she murmured. Picking up a brush, she began the slow process of grooming her horse.

Wyatt frowned. He hadn't expected her to brush down her horse after putting in a full day. "You don't have to do that."

She looked at him in surprise. "You were the one who always pointed out that we couldn't just walk away from our horses after having been out with them like this—not until they were groomed and fed."

Wyatt looked genuinely surprised. "You remember that?"

"How could I forget? You kept reminding me even while I was actually doing it. It was like you felt you had to drum it into my head or I'd somehow forget to do it," she recalled.

"Well, just for today," he remarked with a smile, "consider that piece of information 'un-drummed.' Go to the ranch house."

"'Un-drummed'?" she repeated, amused. "Is that even a word?"

"It is if I say it is," he told her.

"Okay," Bailey said, going along with his pronouncement.

She couldn't resist asking him who was going to take care of the horse she'd ridden today if she wasn't, but before she could do that, Wyatt answered the question for her by calling over one of the hands who happened to be in the stable.

"Hey, Matt, do me a favor and take care of my—" He'd almost said "wife's" but stopped himself just in time. "Of Bailey's horse for her."

"Sure thing, boss." Walking past her, the ranch hand smiled at Bailey. "That was really something to watch today, ma'am." There was genuine admiration in the man's voice.

"Matt doesn't get out much," Wyatt quipped. He tried to keep a straight face but wound up punctuating his statement with a short laugh.

"Can't all be the man-about-town like you are, boss," Matt replied, turning his attention to Bailey's horse.

The ranch hand's words hit her with more force than she thought possible.

Was Matt just kidding around or was there actually someone else in Wyatt's life? He had made it sound as if there wasn't, but maybe he had just glossed over that small fact, wanting to keep that little matter to himself.

He didn't really owe her any explanations, not after all this time, Bailey thought. And he'd had every right to go on with his life after they'd divorced. The fact that she hadn't had been *her* choice and that in no way bound him to pick the same course of action—or inaction, in this case.

Still, she couldn't let go of the thought. It bothered her.

"What's the matter?" Wyatt wanted to know, noticing how quiet she had become as they walked to the ranch house together.

"Nothing."

"Don't give me that," he told her. Stopping for a moment, he looked at her. "I know that face. Something's bothering you. Now, what is it?" His tone indicated that he wasn't about to let her slide.

She was torn between holding on to the lie and telling him the truth. The latter might lead to an argument and, if she made him angry, she could risk losing everything.

But she had never been much of a liar and it was too late to start now. "I don't want to cause any trouble," she admitted.

"What the hell are you talking about?" he demanded. Her choice of words had just fueled his confusion. "Just what kind of trouble are you referring to?"

Wyatt wasn't going to be happy until he dragged it out of her, she thought. So she surrendered and told him. "I don't want to come between you and whoever it is you're seeing."

Bailey's explanation made no sense to him. Wyatt

felt more befuddled than ever. "And just who am I supposed to be seeing?"

"I don't know," she cried, feeling frustrated.

He looked at Bailey as if she'd lost her mind. "Then why are you saying what you just said?" He was curious.

"Because Matt just called you a man-about-town," she reminded him. "And that usually means just one thing."

He frowned. "He said that because he was getting back at me for essentially calling him a stick-in-the-mud. Look, if there was 'someone else,' do you think I would have kissed you...or said I'd let you use me as breeding stock?"

"That's not the way I phrased it," Bailey protested, exasperated.

He suppressed an annoyed sigh. "That's not the point. The point is you seem to think I'd step out on someone I was seeing. Do you really think that little of me?" he demanded.

He was right. That wasn't the Wyatt she knew. Still, she said defensively, "People change."

"I haven't," he stated sternly.

She realized she'd insulted him without meaning to. "I'm sorry," she apologized. "Maybe I'm just being nervous."

It was completely dark by the time they reached the ranch house. He turned the knob and opened the door for her, all the while just looking at Bailey, trying to reconcile what she'd just admitted with the people he felt they both were.

"Around me?" Wyatt finally asked, amazed.

Bailey shrugged. "Yes."

She knew it didn't make any logical sense but, logical or not, it was still true. When she'd initially made her decision to come to Roaring Springs to ask Wyatt to be the father of her child, she'd been convinced it was the right thing. But she'd forgotten to factor in all the other details that were now coming up. Forgotten to factor in all the emotions that were now surfacing.

Wyatt shook his head. "If anything, I should be the one who's nervous."

"You?" Bailey asked, astonished. That made even less sense to her than what she had just admitted to. "Why would you be nervous?"

This was hard for him to confess, but since they were being honest with one another, he forged ahead. "Because you've outgrown me. I watched you today. You were so self-assured and confident, not like the way you used to be when we first came out here. You never hesitated with Annabelle, even though you said you'd never performed that procedure on a milk cow before."

"Outgrown you?" she questioned incredulously. How could he possibly feel that way? "You're a Colton. Whatever you set your mind to, you accomplish. Add to that you're handsome, intelligent and kind." Even more so than before, she thought, keeping that to her-

self. "I'm surprised that some woman hadn't run off
with you the second you were a free man again."

Wyatt frowned. "'A free man,'" he repeated. That
was laughable. "That's not exactly the way I saw myself after the divorce. And maybe the reason no other
woman has run off with me is that I had no desire
to have another woman in my life after you left."
He smiled at her as another wave of feelings stirred
within him. "You're a hard act to follow."

He was only saying that because she'd saved his
milk cow and it was temporarily coloring the way he
perceived things right now, Bailey thought. She was
not about to hold him to anything. And more than
that, she wasn't going to allow herself to believe him,
no matter how much she really wished she could.

Bailey pressed her lips together. He was standing far too close to her, she realized. Turning from
him, she knew she had to create some space between
them before she did something stupid that she would
wind up regretting. He'd agreed to create a child with
her, but if she didn't manage to put a little distance
between them, she was going to wind up making
love with him.

And that would add a whole new set of complications to an already tenuous situation, she thought
ruefully.

She suddenly became aware of the fact that the
silence between them was intensifying. It made her
even more uneasy.

"Um, maybe I should make you dinner," Bailey

said. Turning away from Wyatt, she had every intention of going to the kitchen and doing just that.

But Wyatt caught hold of her wrist, stopping her. When she looked quizzically at him over her shoulder, he slowly turned her around.

"Is that what you really want to do?" he asked in a low voice.

His dark blue eyes held her prisoner. Bailey found that she could barely draw in a breath.

This was ridiculous. They'd been married, for heaven's sake. She knew what it felt like, making love with him. Why was she having these adolescent feelings ricocheting through her like this? Once was a fluke. Twice pointed to an alarming trend, one she couldn't afford to let loose.

But she couldn't lie to him.

"No," she admitted.

Bailey watched, spellbound, as she saw his smile spread from his lips to his eyes.

"Good," Wyatt pronounced. "Dinner is officially on hold."

Before she could respond, Bailey felt his large, powerful hands slip around her face, framing it as if he wanted to examine it more closely.

Her heart began to hammer wildly, slamming up against her rib cage.

She couldn't have moved if she'd wanted to.

And she didn't want to.

What she wanted was to see where this was going.

If Wyatt was going to do what she so desperately wanted him to do.

And then she was no longer wondering because he did it.

He kissed her.

And everything else in the room faded to black.

Chapter 10

This was not the way she had envisioned Wyatt helping her create their child. Not even close.

In all honesty, in the interest of getting Wyatt to agree to father her child, she had thought that in all probability she and Wyatt would wind up making this come about the impersonal way. By that she had assumed Wyatt would deposit his sperm into a cup and she would take that to a fertility specialist to be artificially inseminated. Everything would be accomplished coolly and clinically.

This was neither of those things.

This involved desire, emotions between them exploding. There was an explosion going on inside her, starting from her head going all the way down to the tips of her toes.

She felt *alive*!

Six years was an exceptionally long time to go without feeling alive. But it had taken only moments for her to recognize that special, wonderfully familiar feeling capturing her in its grip.

Wyatt was kissing her over and over again, igniting a fire within every inch of her, making her core pulse with hot, unbridled yearning.

Bailey found herself wanting to rip the clothes from her ex-husband's hard, taut body. But that really wasn't the way she wanted to rekindle this part of their relationship, behaving like a wild, frenzied woman. That wasn't supposed to be part of the equation for her.

Maybe just this one time, she would allow herself to enjoy this, to make love with Wyatt instead of just focusing on making a baby. She knew the latter wasn't something that was going to happen straight out of the gate, not according to what her OB-GYN had told her before she'd set out on this journey to reconnect with her ex-husband.

Wyatt couldn't believe this was actually happening. She felt like heaven in his arms. It reminded him why he had asked her to marry him in the first place. He'd known even then that Bailey wasn't a woman he could just make love with and then walk away from, putting her out of his mind. The exact opposite had turned out to be true. Each time he had made love with her, he'd wanted her that much more.

Regret had only reared its head, taking a huge

chunk out of him, when he'd discovered that Bailey had left him.

But that part didn't matter anymore. Things were different now. And even though he'd had to reconcile some things in his head to forgive her, having her here with him now was all that mattered.

Sweeping her up into his arms, Wyatt began to walk toward the stairs.

"What are you doing?" Bailey gasped, struggling to catch her breath.

"I'm taking you to bed," he answered. "Properly," Wyatt added as he continued walking up the stairs toward his bedroom.

Toward *their* bedroom.

"Properly?" she repeated. And then she laughed softly. "I hope not. I hope there's nothing proper about this," Bailey murmured as she wrapped her arms around his neck and brought her lips up to his.

Wyatt slowed, his progress impeded as he kissed her back with more fervor.

When he heard her moan in response, the sound just excited him even more.

Wyatt didn't remember reaching his room. He was too focused on putting one foot in front of the other, doing his best not to stumble in his eagerness to reach journey's end.

And then he was there, laying Bailey down on his bed, fixating on the next moment.

In less than a heartbeat, Wyatt was there beside

her, continuing to kiss her as he reclaimed every part of her that had once been his to love, his to possess.

Clothes disappeared, replaced with long, languid kisses that branded every inch of her, inflamed every inch of him.

There were no words that could begin to describe how much he had missed this.

How much he had missed her.

He just couldn't get enough of her. Wyatt refamiliarized himself with her body, moving like a man whose long-cherished dream was suddenly, without any warning, becoming a reality.

The more he caressed her, the more he kissed her, the more Bailey felt as if a fire was coursing through her veins, consuming all of her.

She twisted and turned beneath his touch, absorbing the way his warm breath felt along her body, heating it. Making her ache for him. Desperately wanting to make him feel the same way she did.

Bailey suddenly shifted so that Wyatt wound up beneath her. She wrapped her legs around his torso, sealing him to her. It was a movement she recalled that gave him pleasure and giving him pleasure spiked hers to enormous levels.

It felt as if she had never left, Bailey thought, and yet this felt better. Infinitely better. Not just because she had missed this so much but because, somehow, it had evolved to an even more gratifying level.

When she felt his mouth moving slowly along her body, tracing a moist, fiery path to her very core, it was all she could do to suppress the exclamation of sheer ecstasy that threatened to escape from her lips.

This is new, her brain echoed. This was *beyond* wildly pleasurable. She was damp with sweat and determined to take him to the same brink he had just led her to.

Bailey was driving him crazy, taking him a hair-breadth away from sheer madness. He couldn't recall ever wanting her as much as he did right at this moment.

Wyatt didn't think he could last too much longer. His body felt as if it was about to erupt.

His mouth sealed to hers, Wyatt moved her legs apart with his knee. He entered her, moving very slowly to heighten her anticipation and draw out his own. But he could only hold himself back for so long.

Raw, primal urges took over, propelling him on.

He began to move with a growing urgency, each thrust a little more enthusiastic than the one that had come before.

Bailey increased the tempo with each movement from him until they found themselves racing toward a summit that had materialized from the mists, there just for them alone.

With the precision of longtime lovers, they grasped at the stars and felt the soul-jarring explosion together, holding on to one another as the hot sensation bathed over them.

Slowly, by increments, the euphoria enveloping

them receded, leaving feelings of contentment in its wake.

He was whole again, Wyatt thought. For just this moment, just this one instance, he was whole again. He held her to him like a man who didn't want to live in the next moment, only in the one he was currently in. But he knew that wasn't possible. Because the next moment would come. And then the next. And the next.

Wyatt surrendered to the inevitable. "So I guess you'll be leaving soon," he said, resigned to what he knew was coming. His voice echoed in the darkness.

There was only a thin beam of moonlight coming in through the window. But it was enough to illuminate the room. He saw Bailey raise herself up and saw her looking at him quizzically.

"What?" she asked in bewilderment. Why would Wyatt think that? Was he telling her that he wanted her to leave?

Wyatt tried to sound indifferent, even though the thought of having her go hurt far more than he had imagined.

"Well, you got what you came for, so I figure you'll be leaving again," he answered. *Leaving me again,* he added silently.

"Is that what you want?" Bailey asked quietly.

"Doesn't matter what *I* want," he told her. She'd made that clear when she'd left the first time. "You said you wanted me to father your baby and since you and I just did it—"

She turned all the way toward him, stunned as well as relieved. At least he wasn't trying to get rid of her after all.

"And you really think that just one time is going to do it?" Bailey asked incredulously. She shook her head before he could answer her. "Even if I didn't have this medical condition messing me up, it normally takes more than once to make a baby. And given my problem, I'm going to need a lot more help getting pregnant than doing it just the one time." She smiled at him. "No, I'm afraid you're not rid of me that easily."

Under normal circumstances, Wyatt would have made some sort of a pseudo sarcastic comment about being unable to get rid of her, but something Bailey had just said concerned him.

"Just how serious is this problem of yours?" He wanted to know.

She really didn't want to go into it, but she supposed she did owe him some sort of explanation, so she said, "That all depends on what you mean by 'serious.' It makes getting pregnant very difficult."

"That's not what I'm worried about," Wyatt told her. He propped himself up on his elbow to get a better look at Bailey. "Are you in any danger of something going wrong?"

"Something could always go wrong," she answered with a shrug. She didn't want to dwell on that aspect. "This is life."

"I meant if you get pregnant," he said, feeling

that she was missing his point. "Does that put your health at risk?"

"No more than usual." Bailey knew she was sugar-coating it, but she didn't want to say anything that would make Wyatt reconsider his agreement to be the father of her baby. "It's very sweet of you to worry," she told him. "But don't."

She really didn't think he cared, did she? he thought. "Easier said than done," he told her, his eyes holding hers.

Bailey's smile was warmer since they were on the same page—for now. "Maybe I can help you forget about worrying," she said.

Her eyes seemed to be twinkling, or at least it looked that way in the limited light. "How?" he asked her.

Bailey raised her head and brushed her lips against his, lingering for a moment before drawing back just enough to say, "Guess."

Damn but she'd started him going again.

Cupping the back of her head, he brought her mouth to his and lost himself in the sensation he had just rediscovered tonight. The sensation that was ignited by making love with the only woman he had ever actually loved.

"How many chances do I get?" he asked, drawing her body up against his.

"As many as you need to come up with the right answer," she told him breathlessly.

Wyatt had every intention of taking her up on that.

* * *

Later that night, as they lay next to one another, so utterly spent that they could hardly draw a lungful of air, Wyatt asked, "So you'll stay here until you're pregnant?"

She knew that she should put a little space between them, but right now she was far too comfortable just where she was. "That was what I was hoping for—unless you'd rather I move into the hotel in town," she offered half-heartedly.

"No. Given why you came here in the first place, it makes more sense if we're in the same place. And now that I know what you can do—" realizing the way that had to sound to her, he quickly clarified "—with the animals," he told her, "you can help out with the milk cows since there is no local vet and the nearest one is in the next town."

"You're saying that for the time being, I can earn my keep?" she asked, humor curving the corners of her mouth and reaching up to her eyes.

"Well, I wouldn't exactly put it that way," he answered, looking for another way to say it. He didn't want to be insulting or to make it sound that he felt she had nothing else to offer.

Getting a second wind, Bailey quickly cut in before Wyatt could frame his awkward apology. She didn't need an apology. She wanted him to recognize that she could contribute something to the ranch.

"I'd like that," she told him. "I like being useful.

Especially if it's doing the only thing I ever wanted to do."

"Then you were serious?" Wyatt asked. He realized he was being obscure, so he explained. "When you said you've always wanted to be a veterinarian, you were actually being serious?"

"Yes," she answered. "I've always loved animals." She thought he knew that about her. She tried to remember if she'd ever actually said as much to him and couldn't. "It's the one thing I picked up traveling around with my dad." A rueful smile crossed her lips. "Most of the time the animals were nicer to me than my dad was," she said, trying to sound matter-of-fact about it.

"You never talked much about your childhood," Wyatt stated.

At the time they were married, he'd felt that was hers to keep private if she wanted to. But now he found himself curious. There were gaps in what he knew about her. Gaps he intended to fill.

"Wasn't all that much to talk about," she answered, avoiding his eyes. But then she turned her head and looked at him. "Besides, I didn't want you feeling sorry for me. That wasn't the way I wanted you to think of me," she confessed.

"I wouldn't have felt sorry for you," he told her. "So tell me now," he coaxed. "Just so I have a full picture of the mother of my future offspring."

She was reticent. "Knowing I have an affinity for animals should give you enough of a picture."

"And when you *weren't* palling around with animals?" he asked.

"I looked after my father," she said vaguely.

"But he was the parent," Wyatt pointed out. "Shouldn't he have been taking care of you?"

The smile on her lips had a sadness to it that went straight to his gut.

"Not really. Chronologically, he was older than I was, but he never really acted it," she recalled. "My mother left him and he never got over that. When he wasn't trying to ride bulls, he was trying to drink himself into a stupor." She sighed. It pained her to remember those times. "He had more luck with the latter than the former. Too bad the latter wasn't a rodeo event."

Wyatt tried to redirect the conversation toward a better time. "What's he doing these days?"

The smile on her lips was distant. "Not much of anything," she answered.

"Retired?"

"Dead," she answered after a beat.

Wyatt felt terrible that he'd stumbled so clumsily onto the subject. "I'm sorry. When?"

"Five years ago this June," she replied after thinking for a moment. "One of the rodeo clowns found him lying inside the trailer. He was dead."

Maybe if she talked about it, she could put the whole thing to rest. It was worth a try, he thought. "What happened?"

"His heart just gave out. He still had a bottle of beer clutched in his hand." The smile on her lips wasn't bitter, just resigned. "That was his version of dying with his boots on, I guess."

"I am so sorry," Wyatt told her again, his arm tightening around her.

She raised her eyes to his. "I'd like to think he's happier this way. All his rides are a win now."

"No, I meant that I was sorry for you," he told her. "He was your only family, wasn't he?"

What did she say to that? He'd never even referred to himself as her dad. "He didn't think of himself that way," she said honestly.

Wyatt pressed a tender kiss to the top of her head, wishing there was some way he could protect her from the hurt she had obviously endured.

"His loss," Wyatt told her quietly.

Chapter 11

The next morning there was a quick knock on the back door just before it was opened. Hank Wilson looked flushed, but whether it was because he was uneasy about just walking in on Wyatt like this or because there was something else bothering him wasn't clear.

"Sorry to interrupt your breakfast, boss," Hank said. The ranch hand nodded a shy greeting in Bailey's direction. "But you're going to want to see this. You might want to come, too, Doc."

Apparently, Hank and anyone else who had been there for Annabelle's difficult ordeal had now begun to refer to Bailey as "Doc."

Bailey rather liked that. To her it meant that she was fitting in.

"What's so important it can't wait until we're finished eating?" Wyatt wanted to know. It wasn't like the ranch hand to burst in this way, or to even come into the house uninvited.

Something had to be wrong.

Hank shifted uncomfortably. "Maybe it's better if you see for yourself." Pressing his lips together, he added, "You better brace yourself," then advised, "You can follow me in your truck."

Wyatt had risen from the table but stayed where he was. "What are you going on about, Hank?" he asked. "I'm not going anywhere until you start making some kind of sense."

It was obvious Hank didn't want to be the one to say the actual words, but he had no choice. "It's Brahma, boss," he said nervously.

Wyatt looked at this ranch hand sharply. Brahma was his prize bull. The animal had sired some excellent stock in the three years that he had owned the animal. His eyes narrowed as he looked at Hank.

"What about him?"

"Murphy and I found him early this morning," Hank blurted. "We can't get him to come around." Clearly distressed, he looked from Wyatt to Bailey, hoping no blame would land on him.

Wyatt's face grew grim. Breakfast was forgotten about. "Show me."

They followed Hank's beat-up old pickup to the site where he had seen the fallen bull. Murphy was standing over the animal like a distraught sentry, shooing away the crows that seemed bent on swooping in to investigate if not to actually scavenge.

Even at a distance, Bailey could see that the bull's legs were folded up underneath him, which meant that he had to have fallen to the ground. It was *not* a natural position for a bull.

The moment Wyatt stopped the truck, Bailey jumped out on her side and lost no time running to the inert animal.

"Bailey, wait!" Wyatt called after her. "If he's sick, he'll turn on you," he warned. Muttering a curse, he took off after her.

Bailey had dropped to her knees beside the big animal. Ignoring Wyatt's warning, she began to quickly examine the prize bull.

The animal's vital signs were nonexistent, confirming what she'd already suspected. Looking over at her former husband, she gave him the final verdict. "He's dead, Wyatt."

"Dead?" Wyatt echoed in disbelief. "That's impossible. I just saw him yesterday. He was fine," he insisted.

"Well, he's not fine now," she said heavily. "Has he been showing signs of being sick lately? Not eating?" Bailey asked. She was still kneeling beside the bull, running her hand along the animal's hide. He was as cold as the weather.

"Sick?" Wyatt echoed the question she'd asked him. "Brahma's healthier than I am. He's been that way since the day I bought him." He looked mystified and clearly distressed.

"Well, he's not anymore." In a moment of compassion, she squeezed Wyatt's shoulder. And then she looked from the bull to the truck Hank had driven. "Do you think the four of us can get Brahma onto the back of Hank's truck?" she asked Wyatt.

"It'll take more than just four of us," Wyatt told her. "Brahma weighs over two thousand pounds." He looked at her, confused. "Why would you want to load him onto the truck?"

"Well, if he's always been so healthy, then his sudden demise doesn't make any sense. I want to perform a necropsy on Brahma to see what killed him and, more importantly, to find out if he had something communicable that'll put the rest of the herd in any danger."

Hank looked bewildered. "You want to do a necro*what*sy?" he asked.

"It's an autopsy for animals to find out the cause of death," she explained to the ranch hand. She looked back at the bull, thinking for a moment. "Okay, if we can't bring Brahma to the necropsy, we'll bring the necropsy to Brahma."

Wyatt was having trouble dealing with what had just happened. "Once again in English," he requested, torn between being in a state of shock and being just plain angry that this had happened. Beyond the extenuating circumstances, this was going to set him back for a while. Purchasing Brahma had cost him a great deal of money.

"I'm going to go get my instruments and everything else I need to perform the necropsy here."

"You're going to cut Brahma open?" Murphy asked.

The cowboy looked surprisingly squeamish given he'd worked on ranches since he'd turned fifteen years old and had seen and done all sorts of things in that time.

"Only way to do a necropsy," Bailey answered matter-of-factly.

Wyatt nodded. "Hank, take her to the ranch and help her get whatever she needs," he told the senior ranch hand just before he turned on his heel and walked back over to the dead bull.

She felt for Wyatt, but she knew that he didn't like anyone making a point of his softer side. The best thing she could do for him was find answers to what happened to the bull. The sooner this necropsy was done, the better. It would help answer questions.

"Let's go," she told Hank.

The cowboy shoved his hat back on his head and hurried to get into the cab of his truck.

"Well?" Wyatt asked her impatiently.

Bailey had taken over two hours to perform the painstaking dissection. For the most part, he had kept his distance so that he wouldn't get in Bailey's way, but he had watched her the entire time she had conducted the necropsy.

He knew nothing about the procedure, but it was obvious she'd known what she was doing the entire time she'd worked on the dead animal. Never once had he seen any sign of revulsion. She had been extremely professional throughout the whole procedure despite the fact she'd had to remain on her knees while doing it.

He'd wanted to ask questions but had known that he'd be impeding her if he did. So he had bit his tongue and waited. Waited as she'd cut into the bull, sinking her hands, and at times her arms, into Brahma. The bull's blood was all over the heavy plastic apron she'd put on over her clothing.

But she was done now. There was nothing left to take apart. He could see it in her face.

Wyatt wanted answers.

Wyatt *needed* to know what had happened to his prizewinning bull.

Bailey looked up at him, a grim expression on her face. There was no mistaking her findings. "Brahma was poisoned."

Wyatt cursed. Even though he had suspected someone had to have done something to kill the animal, hearing the actual words spoken out loud was like being slammed straight in his gut with a two-by-four.

He looked at her sharply. "You're sure?"

Stripping off the long, blood-soaked gloves, Bailey started to get up off the ground. Wyatt took her elbow and pulled her up, keeping his distance. She stripped off the apron next then shrugged back into her jacket.

"Absolutely," Bailey answered. She pointed out several signs that had alerted her to the bull's fate. She saw Wyatt's face darkening. "Do you know anyone who would do something like this?" she asked her ex-husband. "Is there anyone who's looking for revenge against you or your animals?" She paused. "Or your family?"

He saw Hank and Murphy exchanging looks. As for him, Wyatt was having trouble getting the words out of his mouth.

"I can think of someone," he finally told her.

Color was suddenly rushing up his cheeks. He clenched his hands into fists at his sides, picturing those same hands around the throat of the man he believed was responsible for his bull's death.

"Who?" Bailey cried.

She still knew a good many of the people who either lived in town or near the Crooked C. She was unable to fathom someone doing this awful thing to an innocent animal.

Murphy had no trouble naming the culprit. "Everett Olson, that's who," the ranch hand told her.

Belatedly, Bailey realized that Wyatt was already striding toward his truck.

"Wyatt, wait," she called after him. Quickening her pace, Bailey hurried after him and just barely managed to reach his truck just as he put his key into the ignition.

He didn't turn the key. Instead he glared at her. "Stay here, Bailey."

Her mind was made up. She wasn't going to let him go off half-cocked like this.

"I will not," Bailey cried. "Not when you have that murderous look in your eyes. I'm coming with you," she informed him.

The look in his eyes was dark as he issued the order. "Get out of the truck, Bailey."

"No," she retorted with even more force than before. "*You* either get out of the truck or I go with you. Those are your only two available choices."

Blowing out an angry breath and swallowing a string of curses, Wyatt started up his truck. "Suit yourself, but you're not stopping me."

She was tabling that argument for the time being. "Who's Everett Olson?" she asked.

"The lowlife who owns the ranch next to mine." It was obvious by the way he gripped the steering wheel that Wyatt was doing his best to get himself under control. "He's a ruthless rancher with all the scruples of a rattlesnake. Less," he corrected himself.

Bailey inclined her head, for now accepting the description as gospel. "Okay. And why would he want to poison Brahma?"

"Isn't it obvious?" Wyatt demanded.

"Tell me," she prodded.

"He did it out of revenge," he retorted angrily.

"Olson's been trying to buy up sections of my ranch for the last four years. He wants me out so he can own this whole area. I've turned down every offer he's made and he's not happy about it." Wyatt gritted his teeth, barely controlling the fury building up within him. "He told me I'd regret it the last time I turned him down. I guess that this was what he meant. Killing Brahma was his way of getting back at me."

That seemed like quite a leap to her. "How do you know that?" she challenged.

"Gut instinct," Wyatt snapped. He glanced at her before looking back on the road. "Look, it's best that you don't come along," he said, reading into what she'd just said. "I'll drop you off at the house."

She had no intention of being discarded like excess baggage. "The hell you will," she told him heatedly. "If you think this guy killed your bull—or had someone else kill Brahma—that's good enough for me. But maybe you should take this to the sheriff," she suggested, thinking that a cooler head was needed here right now. "Trey's your cousin and he'll—"

Wyatt's jaw hardened. "I'm not hiding behind Trey," he told her. "I'm perfectly able to handle my own disputes."

She knew that tone. There was no arguing with it. Blowing out a long breath, Bailey settled back in her seat. "Whatever you say, Wyatt. Count me in."

He spared her another look, trying to figure out if

she was humoring him or if she was being serious. He couldn't read her.

"I'd feel a whole lot better if I could drop you off at the house," he reiterated.

"Too bad. I'm coming with you," she informed her ex-husband.

This time, he had no trouble reading either her expression or her tone. Bailey had no intention of budging.

Older than Wyatt by some five years, Everett Olson was half a head taller and at least a hundred pounds heavier than him, if not more. The clothes he had on had a very lived-in look about them and smelled it, as well. When Bailey first saw the rancher, the first words that popped into her head were *gross* and *sloppy*. The words applied to the man's appearance and his manner, both of which were off-putting.

Olson looked less than thrilled when Wyatt appeared in his doorway.

"I don't know anything about what happened to your bull," Olson snapped when his rival accused him of the poisoning. "I've got better things to do with my time than keep track of what goes on at your ranch." He paused to catch his breath, and Olson's small brown eyes slowly washed over Bailey, taking on an almost lecherous glow. "Looks to me like you've got some things going on worth paying attention to, though." The rancher moved so that he loomed over Bailey. "And who is this fine-looking young woman, Colton?"

"Don't look at her like that," Wyatt growled.

"Like what?" Olson asked in a voice that was far from innocent, his attention entirely focused on Bailey. "I'm just appreciating the view, that's all."

Bailey rolled her eyes. She had run into more than her share of men like Olson when she'd been on the rodeo circuit. And she had no problem putting him in his place.

"The 'view' wants to ask you a question," she informed Olson.

The big man leered even more. "Go ahead, little darlin'," he urged. "Ask me anything at all."

"Can you account for your whereabouts yesterday evening?" Bailey had determined that to be roughly about the time the bull had been poisoned.

Olson frowned. "I can. But I'm more interested in what your whereabouts are going to be this evening," he persisted, moving Wyatt aside as he towered over Bailey.

Wyatt had had enough. Not about to be pushed aside, he grabbed Olson's shirt and yanked him away from Bailey.

"She asked you a question, Olson. Where were you last night?" he demanded.

Annoyed, Olson pulled his shirt from out of Wyatt's grasp. "Not that I have to account for myself to you, but I was at the bar in town, drinking for most of the evening. Ask the bartender," he said then added with a smirk, "and then one of the girls at the bar got lucky." He looked at Bailey again because it infuriated Wyatt.

"She wasn't as pretty as you, honey, but I was feeling generous around closing time."

She could see that Wyatt was coming close to losing it. The death of his prize bull and Olson's offensive, boorish manner were about to push him over the edge. Catching hold of Wyatt's arm, she tucked hers through it and turned him in her direction.

"We found out what we came to ask," she said crisply. "Let's go, Wyatt." And then she leaned in slightly, adding in a lower tone, "Please."

Because he didn't want her getting in the middle of what he knew would wind up being a bloody brawl—it would have given him great satisfaction to pummel the foul-mouth rancher—Wyatt turned on his heel and allowed himself to be led away by Bailey.

Trying to distract Wyatt once they got into his truck, she asked, "Is there anyone else who could have poisoned Brahma?"

"No," he rasped. "It's Olson. I know it's Olson, no matter what kind of so-called alibi he's waving around in front of us."

"Well then, we're going to have to find some proof before we can accuse him again," Bailey told him.

Wyatt looked at her, clearly surprised. "You believe me?"

Bailey didn't even have to stop to think. "Yes, of course I do."

It didn't change the situation and it didn't bring back his prize bull, but hearing Bailey say she believed him made Wyatt feel better in a way he couldn't really fully describe.

"We're going to have to stay vigilant," he cautioned her, some of the anger leaving his voice. "Because if Olson is behind Brahma being poisoned—and he is—then this isn't going to be an isolated incident. The guy's not going to back off. There'll be other things going on. We need to keep an eye on the herd as well as the land."

She understood why he was worried about the cattle, but she didn't understand what he meant by the other part. "The land?"

Wyatt nodded. "I don't know what that man is capable of, but I'm not going to just sit back and wind up being ambushed. I intend to stay one step ahead of him or whoever it is he had poison Brahma."

"You're not going to do this alone," she informed him. "I don't like people who hurt animals," she said in case he was thinking of arguing with her.

But he knew better than that.

Wyatt nodded. "Understood."

Chapter 12

She could actually *feel* the tension Wyatt was dealing with. It was there, at the breakfast table with them, like an uninvited guest. It was there, like a pulsating entity, beside them in the daytime as they worked on the ranch, overseeing the cattle. And it was beside them in the dark at night. Bailey shared their old double bed with Wyatt, but nothing else.

Because Wyatt was clearly frustrated that he was unable to bring Everett Olson to justice or to find a way to make the conniving, underhanded rancher confess, Bailey was not about to push her own agenda with her ex-husband. He was in no frame of mind to relax and focus on creating a baby, not when he wanted to exact revenge on a man he considered to be a coldhearted criminal.

But even though the situation regarding Brahma's slaughter was eating away at him, Wyatt still felt that he needed to explain himself to the woman who was beside him in bed.

"Bailey—" Wyatt only got as far as saying her name out loud.

She could hear everything he was feeling in his voice.

Quickly putting her finger to Wyatt's lips, she whispered, "Shh. It's been a very long day, Wyatt. Let's just go to sleep." With that, she curled up on her side and closed her eyes.

Wyatt breathed a sigh of relief. He felt he owed it to her to at least express his gratitude for her understanding. It would be wrong not to. "Thank you."

"Still not sleeping," she responded, pointing out that he was still awake even as she remained where she was.

Wyatt smiled to himself. Bailey could still manage to surprise him.

"Good night, Bailey," he said, turning to his left, the side he favored.

"Good night, Wyatt," Bailey murmured.

Bailey smiled as she slipped off to sleep. Tomorrow would be better, she promised herself.

Wyatt was already awake when she woke the following morning.

"Hi," he greeted her as she opened her eyes. "How are you?"

Bailey blinked then sat up. His question, first thing in the morning, struck her as being a little odd. "All right," she answered cautiously. "Why?"

"You were tossing and turning most of the night and you kept moaning." He reached out to caress her cheek.

She shrugged away his concern. "I was just worried that whoever killed Brahma might strike again," she answered.

That wasn't the only reason. Try as she might to not dwell on it, she couldn't help worrying that she might never have the baby she so desperately desired. Her window for procreation was narrow at best and it was in imminent danger of closing altogether.

However, she wasn't about to lay any of that on him. It would only add to the already heavy mental burden he was dealing with.

"Did I wake you up?" she wanted to know, an apology ready on her lips.

"No, I wasn't having that much luck sleeping anyway," he confessed as Bailey slipped out of bed.

Picking up her clothes from the top of his bureau where she'd left them, she began to head for the bathroom. "Why don't I make you breakfast while you get ready?" she called out from behind the closed bathroom door.

Wyatt raised his voice slightly so she could hear him. "I could get used to this," he confessed.

"Breakfast?" she questioned. "You should. It's supposed to be the most important meal of the day," she reminded him as she came out again, fully dressed. She sat on the edge of his bed to pull on her boots before going downstairs.

"I meant the part about you making it," Wyatt corrected.

Finished with her boots, Bailey smiled as she stood. "You always were the lazy one," she told him with a laugh as she started to leave the room to head downstairs to the kitchen.

"Or maybe I'm just the smart one," he called after her. When she paused for a second to look quizzically at him over her shoulder, he said, "I got you to volunteer to cook, didn't I?"

She made no reply and disappeared from view.

Wyatt didn't know if she'd heard him or if she'd just kept going, ignoring him. In either case, for the first time since he'd seen Brahma lying dead on the ground yesterday morning, Wyatt smiled to himself.

But then, he thought, Bailey usually had that effect on him.

"What do you mean, there's a calf missing?" Wyatt asked Ron Jennings.

The tall, wiry Jennings was another one of his ranch hands. He'd just informed him of their latest problem when Wyatt and Bailey pulled up and asked for a status report on the herd.

"We did a head count, boss, and one of the new calves is missing." He paused for a moment, trying to remember the name that had been given to the calf.

"Daisy," he suddenly proclaimed, pleased with himself. "That's the calf's name." The smile quickly faded when he saw the somber look on Wyatt's face. "We brought them all in last night but she must have wandered off before the barn door was closed."

Jennings looked a bit sheepish as he continued with his narrative. "Her mama was really agitated this morning, making all sorts of noise. That wasn't normal for Buttercup, so I went in to check on her. That's when I saw that her calf was missing."

Wyatt sighed. There was only one thing left to do. "All right, I want you, Lewis and Murphy to fan out and find her. Start where the herd was grazing yesterday."

"On it, boss," Jennings responded, relieved not to get a dressing-down. He went to quickly find the other two hands Wyatt had mentioned.

"I can go look for her, too," Bailey volunteered, speaking up.

"We'll go together," Wyatt told her. When Bailey gave him a puzzled look he said, "I don't want you out there alone. If Olson's out there somewhere, it's not safe for you."

"I can take care of myself," Bailey informed her ex-husband. "I did all those years before you came into my life." He really didn't look convinced. "Not everyone who was on the rodeo circuit was as honorable as you," she pointed out.

He wasn't about to quarrel with her. Time was

essential. The calf couldn't last out there by herself for very long. "Humor me."

Bailey raised her eyes to his. "For most of our marriage, I did," she told him quietly.

He returned her look for a long moment then glibly said, "Then you'll have no trouble remembering how it's done."

Bailey inclined her head. "Okay, we'd better get started."

Because most of the terrain they had to cross was hilly, Wyatt decided they'd make better time taking the horses instead of his truck. It enabled them to take shortcuts.

It was still over an hour before they finally found the lost calf. Or rather, heard her.

Daisy was making a pathetic, almost heart-wrenching bellowing noise.

Wyatt recognized the sound. Daisy was crying for her mother.

"She's that way," Bailey exclaimed as she pointed in the direction of the racket.

"I think I would have come to the same conclusion," he told her, amused she felt she had to take charge.

"You're welcome," she responded, kicking her horse's flanks. Bailey took off, eager to reach the distressed calf.

Wyatt sighed then picked up speed so that he could catch up with her. When they reached the calf, they saw why Daisy was making such an awful sound.

"She's hurt," Bailey cried, dismounting quickly and going to the calf. "What did you get yourself into, Daisy?" she asked as she examined the little animal.

"With so many other calves being born this season," Wyatt speculated, "Daisy probably thought that wandering off was her one shot at getting any kind of attention."

"Calves don't think that way. Daisy's not a person," Bailey told him with a dismissive laugh.

Wyatt squatted next to her to examine the wayward calf for himself. "People shouldn't think that way, either," he finally told her.

He was talking about when she'd taken off, Bailey thought. But she hadn't left him and the Crooked C because she'd wanted attention. The glaring lack of it had only helped her make up her mind to do what she'd felt in her soul she'd had to do.

"Nothing's broken," she announced after carefully checking all four of the calf's limbs and doing a cursory examination of the animal. "She's just a bit scratched up and I think she probably scared herself." She looked at the calf. "Don't do that again, you hear? There's safety in numbers."

As if she understood what was being said to her, Daisy mooed this time.

"I'll put her across the front of my saddle and we'll take her back to the barn," Wyatt told Bailey. "You can clean her up once we get there."

"Sounds like a plan," she agreed, standing.

She got out of Wyatt's way as he rose with the calf. The unexpected motion had Daisy instantly growing agitated again. She started bellowing once more.

"Mama can't hear you out here, honey. Just keep calm," Bailey told the calf in a low, soothing voice.

"I'm going to have to use some rope to secure her," Wyatt said as he deposited the calf beside his saddle horn.

Watching him, she frowned. That didn't look all that secure. "We should have brought the truck," she told him.

"We might not have been able to find her if we had," he reminded Bailey. "Don't worry. This is going to take a little more time, but not *that* much," Wyatt emphasized.

The calf was definitely not happy and made that fact very evident to her rescuers. She kept swishing her tail, something that didn't please Wyatt.

They had only managed to get about a quarter of a mile closer to the Crooked C barn when Bailey suddenly waved her hand at him, wanting Wyatt to stop.

"Stop! Wyatt, stop!" she repeated when he didn't see her waving and just continued.

"Tune her out, Bailey," he advised. "Daisy will be all right as soon as we get her to the barn and her mother."

"No," Bailey insisted, trying to make him understand she wasn't calling his attention to the calf.

"Not her. Look!" She pointed to something lying in the grass in the distance, on her left.

He couldn't make out anything from his vantage point. "Look at what?"

She realized that since he was trying to hold on to the wriggling calf, and she was unintentionally blocking his field of vision on the left, Wyatt didn't see what she did.

"At that!" she cried.

The next moment she was riding toward the form she had barely made out. The form taking on a definite shape the closer she came.

Bailey slid off her horse, unable to believe she actually saw what was right in front of her.

This was awful.

"Wyatt, get over here!"

He was already on his way. The strange note in her voice had him urging his mount on faster, much to the calf's unhappiness.

Daisy started bellowing again.

And then he saw what had gotten Bailey so distressed.

There was the half-clothed body of a young woman on the ground. She was wearing a sparkling dark blue evening dress and was partially hidden by tall, dying weed grass.

"Is she—?"

Bailey nodded numbly. "I think she's dead." She answered Wyatt's question before he asked it.

Hoping to find some signs of life, he needed to get in closer.

"Bailey, put your hands on the calf," he ordered, dismounting. He kept one hand against the calf until Bailey traded places with him. "Keep her from falling off. I tied her onto the saddle, but if she gets agitated enough, she's going to slide off and wind up hurting herself even more."

Bailey nodded, backing away from the body on the ground. She forced herself to look away from the woman. Turning around, she took charge of the calf.

Wyatt knelt beside the woman and felt for a pulse even though her coloring was a disheartening shade of gray. It wasn't just from the cold, he ascertained. Whoever this woman was, she was definitely dead and most likely had been for at least several hours. But that was for the medical examiner to determine.

He wasn't saying anything, Bailey thought, turning around again so she could see what Wyatt was doing.

"Do you recognize her?" she asked.

Wyatt shook his head. "Never saw her before. She might be a local," he allowed, "but I don't see a purse or any other kind of identification."

There was nothing anywhere near the body, nor anything farther away, either. He rose, dusting himself off.

"Do you think that the same person is responsible?" Bailey murmured, unable to take her eyes off the dead woman.

Wyatt wasn't following her. "What do you mean?"

Bailey couldn't see how it hadn't crossed his mind. "There might be some sort of a strange connection between this dead woman and what happened to your bull."

"Why?" He still didn't see how one thing had anything to do with the other. "I already said that I don't know this woman."

"I understand that," Bailey answered. "But she's out here on your property." She looked back at the dead woman. Something occurred to her. "Maybe someone's trying to frame you."

"*What?* That's insane," he retorted, rejecting the idea.

"Doesn't have to make sense to be true," she reminded him. Bailey looked at the corpse as the calf began to squirm even more. "What do you want to do?" she asked. "We can't just leave her here. Whoever did this might be back and he could relocate her body. Or the coyotes might find her, and you know what that means."

"Yes, but we still can't move her ourselves. That would be tampering with evidence and it might just compromise any sort of clues that might be on the premises, not to mention it would implicate us—or at least me—even more." He saw the way she was looking at him. "What? I watch television sometimes," he said. "That's the first thing they're always babbling about on all those cop shows."

"I'm just surprised you'd know something like

that, that's all. You always used to be too tired to watch anything on TV at night," she recalled.

"Yeah, well, when you don't have anyone to talk to, you need something to fill the silence." Clearing his throat, Wyatt looked back at the dead woman. "Go back to the house with the calf and call Trey," he told Bailey. "He needs to come out here."

Rather than do what he said, Bailey looked at him skeptically. "Are you sure you want to be the one to stay out here with her?"

He wasn't sure what she was trying to say. "Why not?"

She shrugged. "I don't know. It might give someone something to speculate on."

Wyatt dismissed her concern. "You're too suspicious."

"I'd rather be safe than sorry," she said. Her gut told her being cautious was the right way to go. "Why don't you take the calf back to the barn and I'll stay with the body?"

"And make you a perfect target for whoever did this in case the guy decides to come back?" Wyatt shook his head emphatically. "Nope, bad idea. I'm not about to leave you here with a dead woman."

She sighed. Wyatt was being overly protective but he did have a point. And after their horrifying discovery, she had to admit she liked the fact that he was looking out for her.

But that did leave them at a standoff.

"Is there a signal out here?" she suddenly asked.

His mind preoccupied with the murdered woman, Wyatt looked at her blankly. "A what?"

"A signal," Bailey repeated, then tried again. "Cell reception," she specified. "Is there any out here?" She took out her smartphone and held it up in front of him.

Now it made sense, he thought. Kind of.

"I don't know. I never carry that thing out here." In all honesty, he regarded quick contact via cell phone something from his old life. It had been a way for his father to always be able to hunt him down. That was part of the reason why he never had it on his person while he was working now.

Bailey jiggled the phone in front of him with a triumphant grin. "Luckily, I do."

Chapter 13

Sheriff Trey Colton didn't say anything for several minutes as he slowly moved around the body, studying the dead woman from all angles.

"Well, she obviously wasn't killed here," he finally said to Wyatt and Bailey.

"What makes you say that?" Bailey asked even though Trey's words had her breathing a small sigh of relief.

"There's no sign of a scuffle anywhere. She was strangled," he pointed out. There were bruises on both sides of her neck, like someone powerful had squeezed the life out of her. "If it was done here, at least *some* of the ground would have been disturbed beyond just the imprint that was left by her body when it was deposited here."

Trey looked at his cousin and Bailey. "How did you happen to find her?" he queried. "All I got on the phone was that there was a dead woman on your ranch."

"One of the calves was missing this morning. We assumed it had wandered off, so we—" Wyatt nodded at Bailey "—and three of my hands went looking for it."

"Looks like you found more than you bargained for," the sheriff murmured, writing down the details in a small worn notepad he always carried with him.

"You can definitely say that," Bailey said, speaking up.

She had not only called the sheriff's office to report finding the dead woman, she'd also called Fox to ask him to take the injured calf back to the barn. She had only contacted Fox after being unable to reach any of the ranch hands she knew carried cell phones with them.

Fox had arrived a little ahead of the sheriff. He hadn't recognized the dead woman, either, when Wyatt had asked him. He'd taken charge of the very unhappy calf and had just driven away with the animal securely tied in the back of his truck when Trey arrived on the premises.

"Do you recognize her?" Bailey asked the sheriff, hoping for a positive identification. She couldn't help thinking that somewhere there was a mother worried about her missing daughter.

"No. Why?" Judging from Bailey's tone, Trey as-

"FAST FIVE" READER SURVEY

Your participation entitles you to:
* ✳ **4 Thank-You Gifts Worth Over $20!**

Complete the survey in minutes.

Get **2 FREE** Books

Your Thank-You Gifts include **2 FREE BOOKS** and **2 MYSTERY GIFTS**. There's no obligation to purchase anything!

See inside for details.

Dear Reader,

Since you are a lover of our books, your opinions are important to us... and so is your time.

That's why we made sure your **"FAST FIVE" READER SURVEY** can be completed in just a few minutes. Your answers to the five questions will help us remain at the forefront of women's fiction.

And, as a thank-you for participating, we'd like to send you **4 FREE THANK-YOU GIFTS!**

Enjoy your gifts with our appreciation,

Pam Powers

To get your
4 FREE THANK-YOU GIFTS:

✶ Quickly complete the "Fast Five" Reader Survey
and return the insert.

▼ DETACH AND MAIL CARD TODAY! ▼

"FAST FIVE" READER SURVEY

1 Do you sometimes read a book a second or third time?   ○ Yes   ○ No

2 Do you often choose reading over other forms of entertainment such as television?   ○ Yes   ○ No

3 When you were a child, did someone regularly read aloud to you?   ○ Yes   ○ No

4 Do you sometimes take a book with you when you travel outside the home?   ○ Yes   ○ No

5 In addition to books, do you regularly read newspapers and magazines?   ○ Yes   ○ No

YES! I have completed the above Reader Survey. Please send me my 4 FREE GIFTS (gifts worth over $20 retail). I understand that I am under no obligation to buy anything, as explained on the back of this card.

240/340 HDL GM37

FIRST NAME	LAST NAME

ADDRESS

APT.#	CITY

STATE/PROV.	ZIP/POSTAL CODE

Offer limited to one per household and not applicable to series that subscriber is currently receiving.
Your Privacy—The Reader Service is committed to protecting your privacy. Our Privacy Policy is available online at www.ReaderService.com or upon request from the Reader Service. We make a portion of our mailing list available to reputable third parties that offer products we believe may interest you. If you prefer that we not exchange your name with third parties, or if you wish to clarify or modify your communication preferences, please visit us at www.ReaderService.com/consumerschoice or write to us at Reader Service Preference Service, P.O. Box 9062, Buffalo, NY 14240-9062. Include your complete name and address.
RS-817-FF18

© 2017 HARLEQUIN ENTERPRISES LIMITED
® and ™ are trademarks owned and used by the trademark owner and/or its licensee. Printed in the U.S.A.

READER SERVICE—Here's how it works:

Accepting your 2 free Harlequin® Romantic Suspense books and 2 free gifts (gifts valued at approximately $10.00 retail) places you under no obligation to buy anything. You may keep the books and gifts and return the shipping statement marked "cancel." If you do not cancel, about a month later we'll send you 4 additional books and bill you just $4.99 each in the U.S. or $5.74 each in Canada. That is a savings of at least 12% off the cover price. It's quite a bargain! Shipping and handling is just 50¢ per book in the U.S. and 75¢ per book in Canada*. You may cancel at any time, but if you choose to continue, every month we'll send you 4 more books, which you may either purchase at the discount price plus shipping and handling or return to us and cancel your subscription. *Terms and prices subject to change without notice. Prices do not include applicable taxes. Sales tax applicable in N.Y. Canadian residents will be charged applicable taxes. Offer not valid in Quebec. Books received may not be as shown. All orders subject to approval. Credit or debit balances in a customer's account(s) may be offset by any other outstanding balance owed by or to the customer. Please allow 4 to 6 weeks for delivery. Offer available while quantities last.

BUSINESS REPLY MAIL
FIRST-CLASS MAIL   PERMIT NO. 717   BUFFALO, NY

POSTAGE WILL BE PAID BY ADDRESSEE

READER SERVICE
PO BOX 1341
BUFFALO NY 14240-8571

NO POSTAGE
NECESSARY
IF MAILED
IN THE
UNITED STATES

◄ If offer card is missing write to: Reader Service, P.O. Box 1341, Buffalo, NY 14240-8531 or visit www.ReaderService.com ▼

sumed she thought he should have recognized the dead woman. "Who is she?"

"We don't know," Wyatt answered. "We were hoping that maybe you did and could give us a name."

Trey's eyes met his cousin's. "Then you weren't with her previous to this happening?" he asked, waving his hand toward the prone body.

"No." There was no room for any argument or doubt in his answer.

"Any idea how she came to be out here?" Trey asked, looking from his cousin to Bailey and then back again.

Trey had always been totally by-the-book without any agenda or ax to grind. While Wyatt could appreciate that, he really wished his cousin was a little more flexible and relaxed.

Wyatt shrugged in response to Trey's question. "I haven't a clue. Maybe you can show her picture around at the Lodge and the Château. Someone might recognize her," Wyatt suggested. "Maybe she was even staying there before all *this* happened." He looked in the direction of the body.

"She could be an escort," Bailey offered, trying to put what she actually meant in polite terms since the woman had been strangled.

Trey nodded as if he had already decided to do what Wyatt had recommended. He pressed his lips together, and his eyes shifted toward his cousin.

Wyatt detected the discomfort his cousin was

wrestling with and braced himself. He nodded, as if urging Trey to say what he needed to.

"I'm sorry, Wyatt, but I have to ask. Where were you yesterday between noon and nine?"

"Is that when she died?" Bailey asked, breaking into the conversation.

"My best guess for now," Trey told her. "We won't know the exact time of death until after the medical examiner has a chance to do his autopsy."

"I was out on the range," Wyatt answered, cutting into the conversation.

Trey made a notation. "Alone?"

"Some of the time."

"But not all," Bailey interjected quickly, stressing the last two words. "Look, Sheriff, you're his cousin. You know that the only things Wyatt's guilty of is working too hard and being too quiet. He wouldn't kill anyone," she insisted.

From the look on his face, Trey clearly agreed with her. "I know that. You know that. But what we believe doesn't matter." He looked at his cousin. "*Do* you have an alibi?"

"Me." Bailey spoke up. "He has me," she said as Trey looked at her. "I'm Wyatt's alibi. We were together."

But Wyatt shook his head, negating what she was telling his cousin. "I appreciate what you're trying to do, Bailey. But no—" Wyatt turned toward the sheriff "—we weren't together the entire time. I went back to check something out." He'd gone back to the spot they'd found Brahma poisoned. He hadn't mentioned that to Bailey and was now debating telling the sheriff.

Trey nodded, taking it all down. "I appreciate you being honest with me, Wyatt. I'll be getting back to you once we have a verifiable time of death," he promised.

Shoving the notepad into his pocket, Trey walked over to confer with the deputy who was snapping pictures of the dead woman as well as the immediate area around her.

"My bull was poisoned," Wyatt told Trey, speaking up suddenly.

Surprised, Trey turned around to look at his cousin again. "Say what?"

"Brahma." Bailey said the bull's name before Wyatt could answer. "Wyatt's prizewinning bull was killed the day before yesterday."

Trey walked back to them. "What happened?" Taking out his notepad again, he turned to a new page and made a couple of additional notes before waiting for more information.

Wyatt gave him a bare-bones summation of the events. "We'd just found Brahma in the field. He was dead. Bailey did a— What did you call it?" Wyatt asked, turning to her.

"A necropsy." Seeing that the sheriff looked puzzled, she explained. "That's an autopsy for animals."

Trey nodded, putting the term down in his notes. "Go on. I'm assuming that you learned something after doing this necropsy."

"I did," she confirmed. "It turns out the bull was poisoned."

"You're sure about that?" he questioned.

There was no hesitation in her answer. "Absolutely."

"Any idea who might have done it?" Trey threw the question out for either one of them to answer if they could.

Wyatt answered. "Oh, I've got an idea, all right. No proof," he added just to cover all bases of the story, "but a definite idea."

"Who?" Trey wanted to know.

"Everett Olson," Wyatt said. "He's been trying to buy up my ranch ever since I got it. Doesn't take no for an answer," he added.

Trey said nothing, only nodded as he made another notation.

"Could the same person who killed his bull also have killed this woman?" Bailey asked.

"Anything's possible," the sheriff answered vaguely. "Right now, we can't rule anything out or just pursue one avenue of thinking. But I'll keep what happened to your bull in mind when I'm questioning people," he promised his cousin.

Trey glanced at his watch then pushed the sleeve of his fur-lined jacket back down into place. "Wonder what's keeping the medical examiner," he said to his deputy. "It's not like there's a whole lot of bodies waiting for his attention."

Bailey saw the dark look on Wyatt's face as he turned away from his cousin. He was anticipating trouble, she thought.

Turning so that Trey couldn't hear her, she asked Wyatt, "This isn't going to go well, is it?"

"A dead woman was found on my property," he said pointedly. "So, no, I'm not all that hopeful that this is just going to go away without generating some kind of repercussions."

"But you said you never met her," she said, restating what he had told her. She believed Wyatt. He had never lied to her in all the time she'd known him.

"No, I didn't. But that won't stop people from speculating and gossiping. And it won't stop them from making accusations."

For his sake, Bailey did her best to sound optimistic. "You never know. They just might surprise you," she told him.

But Wyatt had stopped being optimistic a long time ago.

"I doubt it." He glanced over his shoulder at his cousin, who was talking to his deputy. "Let's go back and see how the calf is doing. There's nothing either one of us can do here," he said to Bailey.

She nodded and they started walking toward their horses.

The look on Wyatt's face was breaking her heart.

"It'll be all right," Bailey told him in the most positive voice she could muster.

He gave her a half-hearted smile that could only be described as being tinged with pain.

Bailey felt for him, mainly when it came to the fate suffered by the bull. But she knew that there was nothing she could say to him beyond what she already had.

She could talk until she was blue in the face, but the only real thing that would help was if Wyatt worked this out in his head himself.

He had never been a happy-go-lucky man, she recalled, but he had never shut down like this back in the earlier days.

Bailey couldn't help wondering if she'd done that to him.

Was her leaving him and the Crooked C the catalyst that had shut Wyatt down to this extent? Had it turned him into a man whose only thoughts were dark ones and who could only anticipate the worst happening?

If his ultimate state of mind *was* her fault, she needed to do something to rectify it, Bailey told herself. Because she really couldn't bear seeing Wyatt like this, like all he could foresee were dark skies and rain because all the sunshine had been banished from his world forever.

Problem was, she didn't know how to bring Wyatt around, how to snap him out of this state.

All she knew for sure was that she wasn't going to leave him until she could figure it out and get him to come around again.

It didn't take long—less than twenty-four hours—for the story about the dead woman found on Wyatt's property to make the rounds.

It seemed like there had barely been enough time for the medical examiner to take the body to Roaring

Springs and perform the autopsy before people were gathering around town in clusters, working themselves up and loudly calling for Wyatt's head.

Wyatt, meanwhile, found he couldn't just stay on the ranch, working. He wanted to find out if any headway had been made in looking for the killer or at least in identifying the murdered woman. He decided to go into town, but before he left he told Bailey to stay at the ranch. He wanted to be sure that nothing happened to her, but she blatantly refused to just docilely obey and stay away.

He should have known she would fight him on this, he thought wearily.

"Don't give me a hard time, Bailey," he told her. "I want you to stay here and be safe."

"Wyatt, we're not married anymore," she reminded him, standing her ground. "You can't order me around and tell me what to do."

He laughed shortly, dismissing her statement as any sort of new protest on her part. "As I recall, I never could."

"Well," she countered, "it's even more so now. I'm coming with you," she informed him flatly, leaving no room for further discussion.

Wyatt sighed. He didn't want to get into another argument with her. Who knew, it might actually be all right.

"All right, you can come—but," he added emphatically, "at the first sign that the crowd is getting ugly, I want you to leave."

"Getting ugly?" Bailey echoed, a bemused expression on her face as she tried to get him to lighten up a little. "Have you *seen* some of the people in this town?"

She saw the corners of his mouth curve in just the barest hint of a smile, which was all she was trying to coax out of him.

"All right," he said, far from happy about surrendering the point to her. But short of getting into a knock-down, out-and-out verbal battle with her, he had no other choice except to acquiesce. "You can come with me."

As if he thought she'd let him leave for town without her, Bailey thought.

Climbing up into the cab, she joined Wyatt in his truck. "Good answer."

It was worse than they had thought. The moment someone had leaked the story about the dead woman found on Wyatt's ranch, the press had instantly jumped on it.

Every word that had found its way online or into print seemed to incense the people in and around Roaring Springs. Boredom and inactivity just seemed to fan the fire. People were out for blood.

The moment Wyatt pulled his truck up in front of the sheriff's office, people began converging around him and Bailey, shouting unintelligible things.

The words might have been unclear, but the mood behind them definitely wasn't.

Wyatt leaned into Bailey and whispered into her ear, "They still have lynch mobs?"

"That's not funny," Bailey retorted. She wasn't worried about herself, but Wyatt was being combative and she knew people didn't respond well to that. The crowd would want to take him down.

"I wasn't trying to be funny," he told her, his expression somber.

Crowd scenes brought out people's baser instincts, Wyatt thought. They always did.

Using his body to shield Bailey as best he could, he hustled her into the sheriff's office. Once inside, he quickly closed the door to keep the crowd out. Only then did he look around the room.

Trey came up to them, locking the door before someone decided to try their luck and barge in.

He turned to look at Wyatt. "What are you doing here?" He seemed truly mystified. "I didn't tell you two to come in."

"I wasn't waiting for you to give me permission," Wyatt answered. Bailey shot him a look and he toned down the hostile note in his voice. "I just wanted to see where you were in the investigation."

Trey frowned in dissatisfaction with his progress. "Same place I was yesterday. There has been one new development, though."

"What?" Bailey asked, excited. Eager to have this resolved and behind them, she was willing to grab on to anything.

"I've got to recuse myself," Trey told them.

This wasn't even close to what either she or Wyatt had been hoping to hear.

"Why?" she asked.

"Actually," Trey explained, "it's in your best interests. People here are all worked up, saying that you're getting preferential treatment because you're a Colton."

"Preferential treatment?" Bailey echoed, incensed. "How is he getting preferential treatment?" She wanted to know.

There was a very simple, if unreasonable, answer to that. "Because he's not in jail," Trey answered.

Frustration all but strangled her airway. "But *he didn't do it*," she cried.

"People think he did," Trey told her. "In any case, this isn't going to go anywhere as long as I'm in charge of the investigation, so I'm handing it over to Daria Bloom." He nodded at the woman he considered to be his best deputy sheriff.

"No disrespect to Daria," Wyatt said, glancing in the woman's direction before turning back to his cousin, "but where are you going to be?"

"Still right here, overseeing the case, but in an advisory capacity. That seemed to satisfy some of the good citizens of Roaring Springs."

"Well, as long as they're happy," Wyatt said sarcastically.

"Don't worry, Mr. Colton," Daria said in her usual calm, reassuring voice. "I intend to do a thorough investigation and to get to the bottom of all this. I'll follow the trail no matter where it leads and find out who killed that girl."

Wyatt knew that protesting wasn't going to change anything. His best bet was to just cooperate. "Ask me anything you want," he said to the athletic-looking, dark-complexioned woman.

Relieved the sheriff's cousin wasn't going to fight her on this, she nodded. "I fully intend to."

Chapter 14

Several ranch hands came forward, gathering together when they saw Wyatt's truck approaching the ranch house. Fox had filled them all in about the dead woman being found on the northern end of the ranch.

The mood among the men was wary but hopeful.

Hank was the first to talk. "Hey, you're back, boss. Everything all right?" He looked as if he was holding his breath, waiting for some sort of a positive response.

Wyatt got out of the truck as Bailey did the same on her side.

"That all depends on your definition of 'all right,'" Wyatt answered. "They still haven't found out that woman's identity or who killed her."

Murphy frowned. Speculation had been rampant

ever since they'd heard about the woman discovered on the property.

"As long as they're not trying to arrest you for the crime, that's all that counts," the ranch hand said.

But that could all change, Wyatt thought. He wasn't about to count any chickens yet.

Because he had always been honest with them, Wyatt told his men the truth. "I have a feeling they still think I'm the chief suspect." Seeing the apprehensive look on a couple of their faces, he tried to say something at least partially reassuring. "But for now, despite the fact that the body was found on my ranch, they haven't been able to find any evidence to implicate me."

"That's because you didn't do it," Bailey said, speaking up.

"What are you going to do?" Fox asked. He'd remained on the Crooked C after having brought in the wounded calf. He'd decided to hang around until such time as Wyatt and Bailey returned.

Glad to see him, Wyatt nodded at his brother. "Not much I can do," Wyatt answered. "I'm just going to keep working on the ranch until something new develops."

"Sounds good," Bailey agreed. "Just tell me what you want me to do."

"About that..." Wyatt began, turning to face her. "Give us a little privacy, boys," he requested, waving off his ranch hands as well as Fox.

"Sure," Hank responded.

"You got it," Murphy told him. Jennings merely nodded, stepping away.

"Okay, I'll be heading back to my ranch unless you need me," Fox told Wyatt. "The calf's in with her mama and she looks better already."

"Thanks, Fox. I appreciate it. You've done more than enough."

Fox waved away Wyatt's words. "You would have done the same for me," he said with certainty before crossing to his vehicle and heading home.

Knowing what a private person Wyatt could be, Bailey waited until they were alone before saying anything.

"Okay, tell me what you want me to do," she repeated, waiting.

"What I want," Wyatt told her, slowly measuring his words, "is for you to leave the ranch."

That was *not* what she'd expected to hear. It took Bailey a moment to recover. And then her face clouded over as she geared up for a fight. "Look—"

Wyatt raised his hand as if to physically stop anything she was about to say.

"Hear me out," he said. "It's not safe for you here with all this potential bad press and even worse feelings milling around. I won't have you putting up with all that," he told her fiercely, talking fast so she didn't have an opportunity to protest. "Once the killer is found and all this blows over, you can come back and we'll pick up where we left off. You know," he added in case she thought he was talking about them having a future together, "making a baby."

"You finished?" Bailey's eyes pinned Wyatt in place.

Feeling he had made his point, he answered, "Yeah."

"Good," she replied crisply. "Because I'm not leaving."

Taking her by the arm, Wyatt drew her even farther aside, closer to the house and away from the others. "Bailey, it's not that I don't appreciate what you—"

She pulled her arm away, her eyes darkening. "I don't want your appreciation, Wyatt. I'm not leaving because I *know* you would never hurt anyone, let alone kill them. If I leave, it'll look as if I'm afraid that you *are* the killer." Seeing him open his mouth, she shook her head. She wasn't finished yet and he needed to hear her out. "I know people better than you think, Wyatt. They'll read into that. And it doesn't take much to agitate a mob. I'm not about to be the one to incite that," she informed him in no uncertain terms.

"Bailey—" Wyatt began wearily.

"Listen, you can talk until you're blue in the face, but you're not going to get me to change my mind. Besides, we all know that you're not much of a talker and I am, so I can outlast you—hands down," she informed him. Taking a breath, she continued. "Now, if you're through trying to lecture me, I have a sick calf

I need to tend to. I'm assuming that Fox put her in the main barn." She looked toward that building now.

Wyatt shook his head at her, surrendering. "For the life of me, Bailey, I don't know whether to throttle you or hug you."

"Well, if I get a vote in this, I vote for the latter," she retorted.

At a loss as to how to get her to do what he felt they both knew was the right thing, he pulled Bailey into his arms. "I should make you leave."

She tilted back her head to look at him. "You and what army?" Then, raising herself up on her toes so that her lips were closer to his ear, she whispered, "It's all going to be all right, Wyatt. Really."

He only wished he could believe that.

"What the hell is going on?" Russ Colton demanded loudly.

The patriarch pushed the front door open and it banged loudly as it came in contact with the wall behind it. Russ took no notice as he barged into his oldest son's house.

It was a day after the body had been discovered and both Wyatt and Bailey had been doing their very best to forget about the drama going on in town. For now, they were going about their work on the ranch as if nothing else mattered.

But apparently everything was conspiring against them, preventing them from being able to block the world out.

About to launch into a lecture full-throttle, Russ abruptly stopped what he was about to say and glared at Bailey.

"You still here?" There was a sharp, displeased edge in his voice before he turned toward his son.

It was obvious the man had already tuned Bailey out, not interested in her answer even if she was about to give one. Clearly all he wanted from her was to leave his son alone.

Unwilling to roll over and play dead for Russ, Bailey cheerfully responded, "Yes, I am."

She was well aware her cheery display would particularly irritate the man she felt had never treated Wyatt well.

Dismissing her, Russ turned his back on Bailey, instead fixing his laser stare on his son. "You didn't answer my question," he growled.

"Well…" Wyatt began as if he was having a conversation with his father instead of the one-sided monologue he knew was in the offing. "Another one of my milk cows is about to give birth and—"

Russ drew himself up to his full height, glaring at his son with eyes that were known to shoot both thunder and lightning at ten paces.

"I don't give a damn about your stupid milk cows! It's time you stop playing cowboy and come back to where you belong. None of this would be happening if you'd stayed there in the first place," he shouted, the veins in his neck clearly evident.

"And just where is that, Dad?" Wyatt asked cynically.

Russ looked precariously close to exploding right then and there. He was not accustomed to being talked back to or defied. He was used to being obeyed.

"You know damn well where. With me," he shouted. "*Working* with me!" he insisted. "Learning how to take over the empire."

There were his father's delusions again, Wyatt thought. Russ Colton thought in terms of what he had created being an empire and of himself as being an emperor in charge of it all.

"There is no 'empire,' Dad," Wyatt told him. "There's just your company, which I have no interest in working for or even being associated with. I'm exactly where I'm supposed to be," he informed his father.

"And just where is that? Waiting to be arrested for murder by a two-bit sheriff's deputy?" Russ jeered. "Now you listen to me—"

"No," Wyatt said, raising his voice to be heard above his father's. "You listen to *me*. Your overbearing manner is part of the reason I'm even being looked at as a suspect in this murder—"

Russ's eyes widened in furious disbelief. "Oh, so now it's *my* fault?" the senior Colton demanded, astonished and infuriated.

"Yes," Wyatt shouted back. "Your domineering attitude gets under everyone's skin. Regular, law-abiding folks don't react very well to power plays conducted by self-bloated, delusional rich people throwing their weight around. It doesn't intimidate people, Dad. What it does is make them angry," he stated. "Angry enough to look for the slightest flaw, the slightest chink in the armor, so they can take those people down."

"So you're just going to go on herding your livestock on this little piece of land like some dim-witted cowboy?" Russ demanded, utterly stunned. "Damn it, Wyatt, you're too smart for that!"

"No," he contradicted, "I'm too smart to let myself be bullied into doing what *you* want me to. It took me a long time to learn that, but I did. I'm the master of my own fate, Dad, not you," he said with conviction.

Russ's eyes narrowed with barely contained rage. "You're an idiot!"

"Maybe. But I'm my own idiot," Wyatt countered, "not yours."

Russ Colton turned on his heel and stormed toward the door. "Ungrateful young whelp, you deserve everything that you get!" he railed.

"I could say the same to you, Dad," Wyatt called after his father.

He heard the front door slam in response. Hard. The jarring noise reverberated throughout the ground floor of the house.

Wyatt looked at Bailey. "You okay?" he asked, concerned about how she might react to the way his father had treated her.

"Apparently still standing after Hurricane Russ," she answered with a smile. "How about you? He lashed into you pretty badly." Even her father, at his worst, didn't hold a candle to the almighty Russell Colton.

Wyatt merely shrugged. "Nothing I'm not used to," he told Bailey. "My father was never someone I could warm up to. Most of the time, he wasn't even present in my life. And when he was—" he frowned as he remembered different occasions "—he would demand that his offspring behave like miniature versions of him. I think he saw *all* of us as being his representatives and we all had to act accordingly or we'd hear about it.

"He felt that anything we did that was less than perfect reflected poorly on him." Wyatt's smile was bitter as he added, "My father always felt that everything was about him, not anyone else."

Bailey's heart ached for him. "I'm sorry."

"Don't be. It doesn't bother me anymore—unless someone tells me how much I remind them of my father," he said with a trace of sarcasm in his voice.

"You're not a thing like him," Bailey said loyally. "For one thing," she informed him with a lopsided grin, "you don't foam at the mouth when you talk."

That made Wyatt laugh, which in turn made her feel wonderful.

He felt a ray of warmth travel through him. For the first time since they had found that dead woman, he could feel some of the tension finally slipping away from his body.

"I think we have that in common," she told him after a beat.

He wasn't sure what Bailey was referring to. "What's that?"

"Fathers that weren't that much a real part of our lives."

When he looked at her quizzically, she elaborated. "Half the time my father didn't even know I was there. He was just trying to pull together enough money to buy his next bottle of whiskey."

Wyatt shared his own experience with her. "The times mine didn't know I was there were the good times. The times he was home, he'd always tell me where I'd failed, how I wasn't good enough for this 'empire' he had put together for my siblings and me. I think it really bothered him when he realized I wasn't trying to please him. That I didn't need his approval."

She laughed quietly. When he raised a brow, silently asking her to tell him what she found so funny, Bailey said, "My father didn't want my approval. Not unless it came with enough money for a couple of bottles of whiskey. He lived from bottle to bottle." She shook her head as fragments of disheartening memories flashed through her mind like a sad kaleidoscope. "I have no idea how that man managed to get on those horses and hang on for the required time limit."

"All right, you win," Wyatt told her.

"Win?" she questioned. "What do I win?"

"Well, maybe it really isn't a 'win,' but you definitely had a worse childhood than I did. At least I had brothers and sisters and cousins to turn to. You didn't have anybody," he recalled.

"I didn't need anybody," Bailey told him.

Until there was you, she added silently.

She would have said it aloud, but she didn't want to lay that on Wyatt. She didn't want him to think part of the reason she had come back was that she was hoping somehow, somewhere along the line as they tried to create another little human being, they might also manage to create a new life together for themselves.

And even though there was a part of her, deep down, that *did* want to give life together another try, her pride would not allow her to even remotely sound as if she wanted Wyatt to take her back.

So, for now, she just wanted to be supportive, to be there for him during this awful time until whoever had killed that poor woman was apprehended.

It wouldn't hurt to have the person who had slaughtered his bull brought to justice, as well.

"So I take it that I can't get you to leave?" Wyatt asked out of the blue, returning to a subject they had discussed the other day.

"Nope, not even with a crowbar. So stop wasting your time trying," Bailey told him.

She expected him to say something flippant or to just shrug philosophically, telling her to suit herself or something equally as disinterested.

He didn't.

He didn't say anything at all.

Instead he drew her into his arms, and as she looked up at him in mute surprise, he lowered his head and kissed her.

Kissed her so that she felt the impact all the way down to her very toes, which curled inside her boots. Kissed her so that her very soul felt as if it had risen in temperature by at least ten degrees.

Try as she might, there was no way she could remain unaffected or even remotely removed. Wyatt always had a way of setting fire to her soul.

Raising herself up on her toes without breaking contact, she wove her arms around his neck and drew her body up against his.

She wasn't sure why he was kissing her. Maybe it was motivated by the fact that he felt sorry for her or by a sudden sense of camaraderie, of kinship that had sprung up between them.

She didn't know, didn't care. All she was aware of was that she wanted him to go on kissing her for just a little while longer before they had to get back to work.

She became aware of another thing in that breath-stealing moment.

She was in love with him even more now than she ever had been before.

And that, she knew, could be a problem.

Chapter 15

"I've got a name, Trey," Daria announced triumphantly as she pushed her chair away from her desk.

As soon as the medical examiner had forwarded the dead woman's fingerprints to the sheriff's office, Daria had begun to diligently try to match the prints with ones on file in the various databases available to law-enforcement agencies.

Her announcement had Trey's immediate attention. "Our Jane Doe has a criminal record?" he asked, turning his chair in her direction.

"There's just one arrest on the record apparently—maybe she managed to keep everything else off in exchange for 'favors,'" Daria speculated, looking at the computer screen again. "Her real name is Lucy Reese. She was also known as Bianca Rouge. And get this," she said, raising her voice. "Our dead woman is a high-end call girl from Vegas."

"Just one arrest?" Trey asked in surprise. That didn't sound right to him, especially if the woman had been in the business of play-for-pay.

"Looks like she came with a really expensive price tag." Daria scrolled down farther on the screen and read what was in the report. "According to this, the woman who manages Heavenly Nights, the escort service Bianca worked for, only caters to men who count their fortunes in the millions."

Listening, Trey nodded thoughtfully. "You mean like the tourists who stay at the Lodge during the skiing season."

The deputy smiled in response, glad they were on the same page. "My thoughts exactly."

She scrolled down another page. Apparently their dead woman had quite a history, she thought. "There's a photo on file," she told Trey, happy to find something she could use. "Let me print that up so I can show it around at the Lodge, see if anyone there has seen her. Or, more importantly," she amended, "if anyone has seen someone there with her."

"Is the photo a recent one?" Trey asked.

Daria took another look at it. "No," she admitted. "But it's still a lot better than the one that was taken of her at the morgue. Even cleaned up, there is no hiding the fact the woman in the photo is dead. I'd rather that not be the first thing that jumps out at the desk clerks when I question them."

Trey nodded. "Good point," he agreed, returning to the open files on his desk.

As sheriff he felt frustrated because he wasn't able to actively take part in the investigation, but he realized that anything he found that could act in Wyatt's favor would be held suspect because of his connection to the family. He just wanted to find the killer and, hopefully, to clear his cousin's name in the process.

But for now he knew he had to leave that up to Daria.

"Let me know what you find," he called after Daria as she crossed to the front door.

The deputy sheriff raised her hand in the air, wiggling it, as if to let him know she'd heard him. "Will do," Daria promised as she left the office and closed the door.

"Have you seen this woman here?" Daria asked the desk clerk—Colin Wilcox, according to his nameplate—placing the photograph she had taken from the files on the desk in front of him.

The well-groomed man frowned, looking at the deputy sheriff as if she was simpleminded.

"Our guests value their privacy," he replied haughtily, "so I'm afraid I'm not at liberty to disclose that to you." His tone indicated that he experienced no regrets over not being able to help her. "And before you ask," he continued, "we have no security cameras on the premises for the same reason."

Daria kept the contempt she felt for the man under

control and slid the photograph closer to him on the desk. "Would you be more at 'liberty' if I told you that she's dead?"

The desk clerk paled a little when he heard that. "What?"

Daria saw with satisfaction that Wilcox wasn't quite as smug as he had been a moment earlier. There was now a trace of uncertainty and fear in his eyes. She took advantage of that.

"Someone strangled this woman and I'm trying to find out who did it. Now, did you see her here at the Lodge or not?" Daria demanded, her tone more terse than it had been a moment ago.

Wilcox cleared his throat. "Let me look at the photo again."

"Take your time." She pushed the photograph even closer to him. "So?" she asked after he had stared at the woman's face for at least several minutes.

It was obvious that Wilcox felt he was on shaky ground. There had been no protocol for this in his training. "She might have been here."

The information was coming in dribbles and drabs, but at least it was coming, Daria thought.

"All right," she replied tolerantly. "And who 'might' have she been seeing while she was here?"

The clerk's arrogant demeanor had vanished entirely, replaced by a growing case of nerves. He raised his eyes to the deputy's, and his gaze radiated obvious distress.

"You have to understand that he's one of our best guests," he told her.

"I don't care if this 'best' guest periodically walks on water. I need a name, Mr. Wilcox," she told the clerk sternly.

She could see that she had broken through the man's resistance. All she needed to do was to effectively press her advantage.

"He's a European millionaire," Wilcox practically wailed.

"A name," she repeated, her eyes never leaving his face.

The clerk shuddered, as if revealing the man's name caused him physical pain. Daria continued to stare him down.

Finally breaking, Wilcox cried, "George Stratton. It's George Stratton."

"Now, was that so hard?" she murmured. And then her friendly manner faded as she asked, "Is he still staying here?"

A look of horror very slowly etched itself on the clerk's face. "Yes, but—"

He was trying to talk her out of questioning the man, she thought. They were wasting time.

"What's his room number?"

Cornered, Wilcox corrected her. "It's a suite."

"What's his 'suite' number?" Daria restated, her expression telling him she was clearly losing her patience.

Wilcox sighed, accepting defeat. "Number 420," he finally revealed.

"Thank you." About to turn away, out of the corner of her eye she saw the clerk reach for something beneath the desk.

"I wouldn't advise calling him, Mr. Wilcox," she warned, "unless you want to be arrested for obstructing justice."

Sufficiently intimidated, Wilcox quickly withdrew his hand from the phone located underneath the desk.

"I won't call," he promised her.

Daria's eyes narrowed as she looked at the clerk. "See that you don't."

George Stratton was an impeccably dressed man with an impressive physique, given that he was well over fifty. Five-ten with brown eyes and immaculately trimmed iron-gray hair, the rich and powerful businessman clearly took command of every room he entered.

Looking at Stratton now as his assistant/bodyguard opened the door of his suite, Daria wouldn't have thought the man would have had to pay for sex. But then, the millionaire might have had appetites that ran into the kinky and bizarre.

Stratton gave her a long once-over as his bodyguard brought her into the room.

"I'm afraid that you caught me at a disadvantage,"

Stratton told her. "Michaels and I were just about to leave."

"This won't take very long," Daria promised. She produced her credentials then showed him the dead woman's photograph. "Do you know this woman, Mr. Stratton?"

Rather than give her an answer one way or another, the millionaire had a question of his own. "Why do you ask?"

She'd seen just the slightest flash of recognition in the man's eyes before a curtain had descended. Stratton knew the dead woman, all right, Daria realized confidently. "She was found deceased."

Recognition was replaced with surprise before another curtain quickly descended. "Where?" Stratton asked.

"In the middle of a field," she answered, never taking her eyes off the man. "But you would know that, wouldn't you?"

Some of the well-polished composure slipped just a little. "And how would I know that?" he inquired, a steely edge in his voice.

Not intimidated, Daria gave him her take on what had happened. "My guess is that a night of rough sex got a little rougher than either of you counted on. She did something to incense you, and before you could stop yourself, you strangled her, accidentally killing the woman."

"I *what*?" Stratton cried indignantly. "I have no idea where you got your information from, young woman, but someone has lied to you. Why would I do something so insanely asinine after going to the trouble of flying Bianca out here?" he demanded. His bodyguard stepped forward but Stratton waved him back. "Yes, I knew her. Yes, I enjoyed her. No, I did *not* strangle her. That would have been a horrible waste and I make it a policy never to waste a good thing.

"Bianca and I understood one another. In my world, that is a rare thing. I did not strangle her," he repeated with emphasis. "Now," he continued more formally, standing, "if you have no other questions, I have an appointment to keep."

Daria's gut told her the millionaire was telling her the truth. He hadn't killed the prostitute. She was going to need more proof, of course, but for now she would allow him to walk.

Still, she felt she needed to warn him. "Don't leave town, Mr. Stratton."

"I have no plans to leave for a week," Stratton replied. "After that, if you have any further questions, you will have to reach me in Zurich." He took a card from his breast pocket and held it out to her. "Here is my number."

His tone was dismissive, telling her that he had spent enough time with her and the subject no longer interested him. She didn't care for his tone, but she couldn't arrest a man just because his attitude ticked her off. Daria accepted the card.

She left the Lodge shortly after that. Daria still disliked the man, but she was no longer focusing on him as a murder suspect. Stratton didn't strike her as the type to kill anyone. It was way too much of a bother.

However, she did make a mental note to look into his bodyguard—just in case. There was always a chance that Michaels might have killed the call girl at Stratton's behest.

Daria sighed as she crossed to her car. She had the woman's name and where Bianca had been, at least for a night, but she had nothing else.

Still, it was a start.

Wyatt couldn't just sit on his hands any longer. He had tried to divert his mind to keep himself occupied, but it was impossible to really focus on anything else while this possible murder charge loomed over his head.

Giving in, he called Trey, hoping to find out if the deputy he had put in charge of the case had found out anything.

Wyatt had never been good at small talk, so he came right out and asked his cousin the question festering in his mind for a day now. "Did your deputy find out anything about the dead woman?"

"Wyatt, you know that I can't divulge—" Trey began.

Wyatt cut his cousin off before he went any further. He wasn't in the mood for excuses.

"Trey, this is my life we're talking about," he stressed. "I can't just sit here, waiting until one of you decides it's okay to tell me something. I need to *know*," he insisted.

Trey sighed then relented. "She's got a name," he told his cousin reluctantly.

"Go ahead," Wyatt urged. When Trey didn't say anything further, Wyatt felt his impatience spiking. "Those people in town the other day were ready to condemn me for murder on the spot. I need to clear my name and I can't wait for someone else to do it at their own pace now that you've been sidelined— no offense to Daria."

Sympathizing, Trey gave in. "The dead woman's name was Lucy Reese. She had an alias—Bianca Rouge."

"An alias?" Wyatt repeated. "Was this woman a criminal?" Wanting to know, he'd said the first thing that came to his mind.

"Let's just say she was a lady of the evening. A high-priced lady of the evening," Trey emphasized. "Someone paid to fly her out from Vegas."

Now they were getting somewhere, Wyatt thought. "Anything else?"

"Daria went to find out if anyone at the Lodge had seen her, but she isn't back yet— Wyatt? Wyatt, are you still there?" he asked.

But Wyatt had hung up. He'd heard what he'd needed to hear. That the murder victim had a name and there was a starting point for the investigation.

The Lodge.

He made a point of avoiding Bailey as he began to

leave the house. He had no idea what he was going to find out and he wanted to keep her safe and away from this whole sordid mess at all costs. He intended to conduct his own investigation at the Lodge.

Decker was the manager there. He planned to talk to his younger brother to find out whatever information he could about this dead prostitute.

At the very least, he was certain that now there would be another suspect in the offing. If the woman was a prostitute, that meant there had to be at least one john to question, if not more.

Wyatt had almost gotten to his truck when Bailey suddenly appeared out of nowhere and accosted him. "The calf is almost completely healed," she announced happily. "It's like her injury never even happened." Belatedly, Bailey realized she'd stopped Wyatt from getting into his truck. "Where are you going?"

Several excuses filtered through his brain. He was tempted to give her one of them, but he didn't want to be caught in a lie. When they'd initially been together he hadn't lied to her and he really didn't want to set a precedent now.

So, with no other option left, Wyatt told her the truth. "I'm going to the Lodge."

Bailey was instantly alert, putting two and two together.

"Did you find out anything about that woman who was killed on your property? Was she a guest there?" Bailey asked, eager to have this all resolved once and for all. As far as she was concerned, it was already taking too long.

He looked at her in surprise. How had she guessed? "What makes you think that?"

"Because you wouldn't just pick up and go to the Lodge in the middle of the week for no reason," she pointed out.

"Maybe I just wanted to see Decker," he told her, clutching at the first excuse that came to him.

"Why? Was he involved with that woman? Did he know her?"

Bailey was like a dog with a bone, he thought. Apparently he wasn't going to be able to leave without at least telling her something.

"That's what I'm trying to find out," he told her. "I called Trey to see if his deputy had found anything out," he added. "Turns out that the dead woman's fingerprints are in the system."

"As a government employee or because she was arrested for something?" Bailey inquired.

He hadn't even thought of the first thing she'd mentioned. That just proved to him that Bailey was always thinking.

"Definitely not a government employee," he assured her. "Turns out the dead woman was a high-end escort."

"A call girl," Bailey concluded. She scrutinized Wyatt. "There's more, isn't there?"

"She was flown out from Vegas by one of the guests staying at the Lodge."

"So what are we waiting for? Let's go," she urged, opening the passenger-side door of the truck.

"I was hoping to go alone," he told her bluntly.

"And I was hoping to be five foot six. Not going to happen—in both cases," she informed Wyatt. "Now, we're wasting time. Let's go see your brother," she said, getting into the truck.

After a beat, he gave up and climbed in on his side.

Chapter 16

A year separated Wyatt and Decker Colton with Wyatt being the older of the two, but they might as well have been twins. Both men had dark brown hair, although Decker wore his short and neatly styled while Wyatt's hair was on the long, shaggy side. Both men were tall and impressively well built. The only visible difference between the two was the color of their eyes. Wyatt's eyes were decidedly dark blue while Decker's were dark brown.

Both brothers had nice smiles, too, Bailey observed. However, those smiles were usually effectively hidden beneath scowls.

Decker was wearing a scowl now as he saw Wyatt cross the lobby of the Lodge, apparently headed straight for him. The fact that his brother's ex was with Wyatt just added confusion to the situation.

A situation he had no time for.

Reaching his brother, Wyatt asked, "Decker, got a minute?"

It was obvious to anyone who looked that Decker was harried.

"As a matter of fact, I don't." Making a notation on the ledger one of the clerks held out to him, Decker said, "Listen, if you need to discuss something, why don't we make an appointment for later on today or, better yet, tomorrow?" He nodded at the ledger he'd just signed. The clerk withdrew with it. "I'm really busy right now." Decker offered Bailey what might have passed as a smile, but it quickly faded as he began to turn away.

"Later on today or tomorrow isn't acceptable, Decker," Wyatt informed his brother. "I need to talk to you *now*."

Decker's scowl grew deeper. With an exasperated huff, he gestured Wyatt and Bailey toward his office.

Once there, Decker said, "Make it quick. Like I said, I'm really busy today."

"Maybe you haven't heard," Wyatt began, a touch of sarcasm entering his voice, "but there was a dead woman found on my property the other day."

"I heard," Decker answered almost dismissively and then paused to look at Wyatt. "You didn't do it, did you?" It wasn't a question but more of a rhetorical statement.

"No, I didn't," Wyatt snapped, his voice tight. "But that doesn't stop a lot of people from thinking that I did."

"It'll blow over," Decker said, giving the topic no more attention than a discussion about the weather. As he spoke, the manager of the Lodge began looking through several folders on his desk, arranging them in descending date order.

Wyatt put his hand on top of the folders, forcing Decker to stop reviewing them and bring his attention back to the matter he had just raised.

Decker looked at him impatiently, waiting.

"According to what Trey's deputy found out, the woman was here at the Lodge before she died. Rumor has it she was 'visiting' one of your guests," he said, throwing the term out loosely. "Do you know anything about that?" His eyes pinned Decker in place.

Appalled, Decker glowered at his brother. "Lower your voice," he snapped. "There are a lot of well-known, rich people who stay here. You start poking around and they'll take their business elsewhere. This isn't the only place in Colorado with snow," he reminded Wyatt. "Business starts dropping off and Dad's going to have a fit."

Wyatt stared at his brother in disbelief. "Is that what's important to you? Keeping *Dad* happy?" he demanded incredulously.

Decker lowered his voice even more. "Look, you don't understand. I'm under a lot of pressure here, Wyatt. Dad's dangling the keys to the CEO position over my head. Everything I do is being examined under a high-powered microscope. A major scandal will blow everything sky-high. Even a minor one," he amended.

In this particular case, Wyatt had no sympathy for his brother.

"One way or another, Dad's been doing that with all of us for years. The man is a control freak, Decker," he stressed. "He wants us to dance to whatever tune he plays for as long as he plays it. It feeds his ego."

"I know, I know," Decker retorted. "But—"

Unable to remain quiet any longer, Bailey felt she had to say something. The circumstances here could have a direct effect on Wyatt.

"There shouldn't be a 'but,'" she told her former brother-in-law. "This isn't just a reputation we're talking about. This is Wyatt's life. How is it going to look for 'business' if Wyatt's arrested for that woman's murder?" she asked Decker. "Dragging the family name through the mud isn't going to put the Lodge on the map, at least not in a good way. It'll have the exact opposite effect." She released a sharp breath. "Wyatt's your brother, Decker. You should be doing everything you can to help him clear his name without even *thinking* about what it means in terms of the business."

"I see you brought your attack dog along," Decker said to his brother. The corners of his mouth curved just a little as he saw Wyatt was about to say something. Decker beat him to it. "No, she's right. I'm sorry. Day-to-day dealings with Dad have me on edge and not thinking clearly. Let me see what I can find out for you—and I will get back to you. I'll call you later today," he promised. "If I don't, you call me."

"I'm going to take you up on that," Wyatt told his brother. His eyes met Decker's. "You know I will," he added.

"I know." He also knew that Wyatt didn't say things just to hear himself talk. "And again, I'm sorry."

"Don't be sorry," Wyatt told him. "Just get me all the information you can about Bianca Rouge."

The mention of the woman's name immediately caught Decker's attention. The hint of an emerging smile receded. "What did you say her name was again?"

"Bianca Rouge," Wyatt repeated, watching his brother's reaction. Something was up. "At least, that was the name she was using."

"Damn," Decker muttered under his breath.

"You do know her," Bailey concluded.

"Not personally or by sight," Decker explained. "But I do know that one of the guests told me he was expecting a woman named Bianca and to send her up to his suite when she arrived. She was coming here from Las Vegas."

They were talking about the same woman. "Bingo," Wyatt declared.

"Who was the 'guest' who was waiting for her?" Bailey asked Wyatt's brother.

Decker sighed. "George Stratton." The manager of the Lodge instantly made his appeal. "Wyatt, the man's a high roller. Stratton oozes money. He's worth millions. Half the people staying here are here because of his recommendation. You better not insult him, Wyatt."

"I'm not planning to insult him," Wyatt reassured his brother. He was *not* about to be talked out of this. "I'm just planning to ask him a few questions."

It was obvious that his brother saw no way out. "Oh, all right," Decker said, giving in. "I'll come with you."

"No," Wyatt said firmly, vetoing the idea. "You won't. You'll stay here." Decker began to protest but Wyatt made his case. "I can't ask him questions if you're standing there, apologizing to him for my every word. At the very least, he'll clam up."

"But—"

"I'll go with Wyatt," Bailey volunteered, looking at Decker.

"See? I'll have my 'attack dog' with me. She's just as apt to turn on me as she is to back me up," he told his brother. "Does that satisfy you?"

Decker was not a happy man. "Not really," he answered. "But I suppose it'll have to do." Narrowing his eyes at Wyatt, he said, "Just be diplomatic when you talk to Stratton."

Wyatt frowned. "Just how do you 'diplomatically' ask a man if he killed somebody?" Wyatt deadpanned. "I'm open to suggestions."

Decker gave him a dark look that made his displeasure abundantly clear.

"One more thing," Wyatt remembered to ask just as he was about to walk out of his brother's office.

Decker looked at him, waiting for the other shoe to drop.

"What's the number of Stratton's suite?"

Decker hit a couple of keys on the keyboard and opened the window with all the Lodge's current registration information.

"Suite 420," Decker told him.

"Thanks," Wyatt said just before he left the room.

A man on a mission, Wyatt headed straight for the elevator.

Bailey fell into step beside him. "Your father really cracks a whip, doesn't he?" she commented, thinking of Decker's initial reaction to Wyatt's questions.

Wyatt pressed for the elevator. The expression on his face was hard as he shrugged at her observation. "It makes him feel powerful."

But not loved, Bailey thought. She wondered if the man even realized what his plays for authority ultimately cost him.

"That's really sad," she said. She couldn't help thinking of the way all this had affected Wyatt when he was growing up.

They'd both had things to overcome, she thought.

"I know." The corners of his mouth curved in a cryptic smile just for a moment as he looked at her. "I'm a real disappointment to him."

The elevator arrived and they got on.

"If that's how he feels," Bailey told him, "that's his problem. Because you're your own man and you should be proud of that. He should be, too."

Wyatt didn't answer; he merely smiled.

"So? What do you think?" Wyatt asked Bailey forty minutes later as they walked out of the millionaire's suite.

She was relieved to be out of there. The man had kept looking at her as if he was envisioning stripping her out of her clothes. He'd never said anything to that effect, but he hadn't had to. His eyes had said it for him.

"I wouldn't want to spend an afternoon with that guy. But, to be honest," she told Wyatt after a moment's reflection, "I don't think he's the one who killed Bianca."

Wyatt nodded. "I don't, either," he agreed.

Much as he would have wanted Stratton to be the guilty party, the millionaire didn't strike him as someone who would waste his time killing someone who displeased him one way or another. He would have just told her to get out and then had another woman sent in her place. It was obvious that, as far as Stratton was concerned, people were interchangeable entities.

Psychopaths killed people who annoyed or displeased them for real or imagined reasons. Stratton didn't seem like a psychopath to him.

"So now what?" Bailey prompted.

"Now we go see Daria and find out if she has anything more to go on," he answered.

It wasn't exactly proactive, but it was all he could think of doing at the moment.

Daria wasn't in the sheriff's office when they got there.

"She's out following up on some anonymous tip she got," Trey told them when Wyatt asked after his deputy.

"What sort of tip?" Bailey wanted to know.

"I have no idea," Trey answered honestly. "She didn't want to talk about it in case it fell through. So I didn't push it." He shrugged. "Everyone's got their own style when it comes to investigating a crime, and I've learned to trust Daria's instincts." He looked from his cousin to the anxious woman beside him. "If Daria manages to unearth anything worthwhile, you'll be the first to know," he promised. He saw the reluctance in his cousin's face. "Go home, Wyatt. You've got a ranch to run, remember?"

Wyatt relented. There was no arguing with that. He knew he had already allowed this whole matter to consume him more than it should. It had also taken up more of his time than he was happy about.

"Yeah, I do." He paused by the door. "The first to know?" he asked, just wanting to hear his cousin's reassurance one last time.

"Before she even has a chance to finish talking to me," Trey assured him.

Wyatt still wasn't happy about the situation but he resigned himself to it.

"Guess that'll have to do," he said. With that he escorted Bailey out of the sheriff's office.

Wyatt was silent for the first ten minutes they were in his truck, heading for the Crooked C. And then, out of the blue, he glanced in her direction.

"An attack dog, huh?" He pretended to give her a once-over. "I guess I can see the resemblance," he allowed.

Bailey wasn't sure just how she should take that. "What?"

"In your manner, not your looks," Wyatt quickly corrected. And then he smiled at her, relaxing a little. "You were pretty good in there with my brother. I think you got him to see the error of his ways. That's more than anything I ever managed to do."

She sincerely doubted that. "He would have come to the same conclusion, Wyatt. It just might have taken him longer."

"Don't belittle your contribution in all this," he chided. "You're what keeps me grounded," he admitted after another minute.

About to shrug off the praise, she changed her mind just before she uttered the words. Instead she inclined her head, a warm smile on her lips. "Glad I could be of help."

"And I'm glad you came back, Bailey," he admitted gruffly. He thought of everything that had happened in the last couple of weeks. "This would have been hell to put up with alone."

"But you're not alone," she insisted, surprised he should feel that he was. "You've got Fox and Trey in your corner—*and* your men." And then she laughed to herself.

"What's so funny?"

"There's also your father," she said, doing her best to try to maintain a straight face. "He looked ready to take on the whole world in your defense."

"Right. In exchange for my soul," Wyatt retorted. "Don't let those expensive clothes he wears fool you," he warned. "Under those designer suits and custom-made shirts beats a heart carved out of stone. All that man was ever interested in was keeping the Colton name above reproach to preserve his own legacy.

"He talks about grooming us to take over someday, but the man has no intentions of *ever* dying and letting that happen. He really does intend to go on forever, pulling our strings and overseeing our lives until we're the ones who die, not him."

"I wonder if they can get that into a Father's Day card," Bailey said as if actually thinking out loud.

The simple sentence, uttered in such a straightforward manner, had Wyatt laughing so hard, he had to slow his truck down because he was afraid he'd wind up driving the vehicle off the road and into the nearest ditch.

Pulling over and yanking the hand brake, he stopped the truck altogether.

"I needed that," Wyatt told her honestly, referring to his reaction to her comment.

And then his expression sobered. His eyes roamed her face as if he hadn't already memorized every inch of it over and over again in his mind.

"And more than that," he continued in a far huskier voice, "I needed you. I *need* you," he corrected.

He didn't mean that, Bailey told herself as her heart skipped a beat. It was just the stress of everything he was enduring at the moment. Once this murder investigation was cleared up, Wyatt would go back to being himself, a self-enclosed man who needed no one and wouldn't allow anyone in.

She needed to remember that.

Chapter 17

Any thoughts of spending some quality intimate time with Wyatt vanished the moment they arrived at the Crooked C. They'd gotten as far as the main barn before they saw Hank and Murphy making a beeline for Wyatt's truck.

Hank looked relieved to see them. Or, more specifically, her. "Doc, Elvira's not doing well," the foreman called to Bailey before she even had a chance to exit the truck.

"And we found another injured calf," Murphy told them, his voice merging with Hank's.

"Another one got out?" Wyatt asked, surprised as he got out of the truck.

This didn't sound like a coincidence. One calf escaping could be seen as an oversight or an accident. Two began to sound as if something else was going on.

"Yeah. We found her pretty far out but she wasn't really hurt that bad," Murphy said. "Just some cuts and bruises."

"What's wrong with Elvira?" Bailey asked as she approached Hank. Elvira was one of the milk cows that was currently pregnant.

"I think she's having the calf now," Hank told her as he led the way to the barn.

"That's not possible," Wyatt protested. "She's only eight months along. She's not due yet." Cows had a slightly longer gestation period than humans, taking any time between nine and a half to ten months to give birth. This was way too soon.

"Tell that to her. She's doing all the same things that Annabelle did just the other week." Murphy shrugged helplessly. "I dunno—maybe she's having sympathy pains," he said.

"Cows don't have sympathy pains," Bailey told the men.

She walked into the barn. Elvira was in her stall, just as agitated as Annabelle had been the other week.

Bailey performed a quick exam on the cow and wasn't happy with her findings. "You're right," she told Murphy. "It looks like she's going to have that calf." Bailey frowned. "I just don't know if the calf's going to survive being born this early."

"What do you need?" Wyatt asked, ready to help any way he could.

Bailey dragged her hand through her hair as she looked at the cow. "Prayers wouldn't hurt," she answered absently, thinking.

And then Bailey squared her shoulders and began issuing orders, asking for towels and basins of water along with anything else that came to mind. She wanted to get the milk cow calm and comfortable if at all possible. The less agitated Elvira was, the better for both her and her unborn calf.

It was a long, grueling ordeal, or at least it felt that way to Bailey. But finally Elvira gave birth. The newborn calf looked almost like a smaller, inanimate version of the real thing.

"The calf's not moving," Wyatt realized as he looked at it, disappointment echoing in his voice. "Bailey?"

"Get me more towels!" Bailey ordered as she rubbed her hands along the small calf's damp body, trying to get its circulation going. "Wyatt, keep rubbing her," she instructed as she suddenly began to rummage through her medical bag.

Wyatt was quick to do what she told him to. The animal's flesh felt sticky to the touch but he kept rubbing, trying to make the calf come around.

"What are you looking for?" he asked, imitating all of Bailey's movements and watching the calf closely for a response.

"This," Bailey cried, removing what, for all intents and purposes, looked like a large turkey baster.

Wyatt and Hank stared at the object as she took it out.

"What are you planning on doing with that?" Wyatt wanted to know.

"I'm going to clear out all her passageways," Bailey answered as she inserted the tip of the instrument first into each of the calf's nostrils, then down her throat. Squeezing the rubber bulb, she carefully extracted globs of mucus and other waste.

When she cleared its throat, the calf began to move very weakly.

The ranch hands had crowded around the calf and Bailey. They watched her as she worked. No one spoke or even breathed.

"She's moving!" Murphy declared excitedly. "We got her back!"

"Atta girl, stay with us," Bailey coaxed. "You're doing fine. Just keep on doing it. Your mama wants to meet you," she told the calf.

It took some time to clean the calf up and a little more time before the newborn could stand on her own very wobbly legs. Once that happened, mother and calf were finally reunited.

"We'll call her Gargantua," Wyatt said, awarding the calf the extremely whimsical name. When Bailey looked at him curiously he said, "Because she's got such a huge spirit."

Pleased with how all of this had turned out, he

grinned as he turned to Bailey. One look at her face and his grin faded. "Hey, are you crying, Bailey?"

"No. Yes." She waved her hand at his question but couldn't deny it now that he had seen her face. "I always get misty when a little guy makes it against all odds," she replied, wiping the back of her hand against her cheeks.

Wyatt put his arm around her shoulders and helped her to her feet. There was sympathy in his eyes. "You must be exhausted."

Ordinarily she would have denied Wyatt's assessment. But she was honestly too tired to effectively lie. So she admitted, "I'm ten steps past exhausted and on my way to dead."

"Not on my watch," he told her. He continued holding Bailey, afraid that she might collapse if he let her go.

She struggled to regain some strength in her limbs. She'd spent a lot of time crouching and kneeling beside first Elvira and then her calf.

How long had she been in the barn? Bailey had lost track at this point. "What time is it anyway?" she asked.

"Long past your bedtime," he told her. "Long past everyone's bedtime." He glanced out the window, judging that dawn wasn't all that far away. "It's actually almost time to get up again."

"Oh, good," she sighed. "I guess that since I'm on my feet and dressed, I'm ahead of the game."

He ignored her comment. "You're going to bed," he informed her.

Bailey looked at him, regret flooding her. She wanted to be an active participant in their lovemaking, not just a passive recipient.

"Oh, Wyatt, I don't think I'm up to—"

He realized what she had to be thinking and quickly corrected the misunderstanding. "I meant alone. You need your rest." He looked at her closely. "You looked *really* tired."

She knew he was right. But she just needed her batteries recharged and that shouldn't take much time. "I'll just grab a couple of hours..." she began.

The next minute Bailey found herself being lifted into Wyatt's strong arms.

He vetoed her time limit. "You'll grab a full eight hours," he informed her. Then he began to walk toward the house with Bailey in his arms.

"We'll compromise," she countered, even though every bone in her body wanted to curl up against his big, broad chest and drop off to sleep. "Four hours."

"Six," Wyatt said.

"Five."

He laughed as he shook his head. They were almost at the house. "All right," he agreed, "five. But not a minute less."

Bailey stifled a yawn as she said, "Deal."

She was asleep before they ever reached the master bedroom.

"You are a stubborn woman, Bailey Norton Colton,"

Wyatt whispered to the sleeping woman in his arms. He slowly laid her down on the bed. "I guess that was one of the things I always liked about you."

He decided not to risk waking Bailey up by taking off her boots. So he just drew the covers up over her and brushed a tender kiss against her cheek before tiptoeing out the room.

Tired himself, Wyatt sacked out in the guest room. When he laid his head down on the pillow, he discovered it still had her scent. He took in a deep breath, allowing it to drift through him.

Bailey was the last thought he had before he fell asleep.

Daria had come up against several dead ends in her ongoing investigation to find Bianca's killer. Because of that, she fully expected this latest "tip" to lead to the same ultimate destination.

Still, no stone unturned, she told herself, knocking on the motel room door the newest tip had brought her to. The motel was one of those rent-by-the-week places meant to offer temporary respite for those folks who were just passing through on their way to somewhere else.

This particular room was the temporary home of Nolan Sharpe, a low-level criminal who had been in and out of prison a couple of times, serving time for theft. He wasn't a very skillful thief but he was obviously determined to get better at it if his rap sheet was any indication.

When there was no answer to her knock, Daria tried again. She thought she heard a low moan in response, but then nothing more.

"Mr. Sharpe, are you in there?" she called through the door. This time there was nothing, but she was sure she had heard something when she had knocked that second time.

Doubling back down the stairs, she went to get the clerk at the registration desk.

Howard Emerson, a fixture behind the desk for too many years now to count, clearly wasn't happy about being asked to leave the game he was watching on his TV monitor. And at close to three hundred pounds, the five-foot-nine, balding man with the nondescript eyes clearly preferred being stationary.

"You can always just give me the key," Daria told him.

"Here," Emerson said, holding out the key as he continued watching the game as if every moment was critical. "Knock yourself out."

"Great work ethic," she muttered, though she doubted the man had even heard her. If he had, he gave no indication.

Daria retraced her steps to Sharpe's motel room. Slits of light were visible through the spaces where the bottom of the door didn't quite meet the doorsill. The sagging drapes were drawn across the window, so she wasn't able to look in.

She knocked one last time. "Open the door, Mr. Sharpe, or I'm going to be forced to open it myself."

She gave the man to the count of five in her head. There was still no response. Left with no choice, she put the key into the lock and slowly turned it. Removing the key, she dropped it into her pocket and took out her service weapon. It was better to be prepared than caught off guard. She'd learned that early on.

Using the tips of her fingers, she slowly pushed the door open.

There was only one lamp on in the room and the light it provided was dim, giving a mournful-looking cast to the room.

It turned out to be appropriate, given what she saw next.

Nolan Sharpe was lying slumped over and face-down on the motel floor. There was a gun beside him on the right and a note on his left.

There was also a bullet in his right temple.

It appeared that Nolan Sharpe had committed suicide. Not very skillfully, she thought, if he was the one she'd heard moaning when she'd called out to him. One well-placed bullet should have been the end of it.

Obviously the man's aim was a little off.

Daria quickly checked the bathroom and the closet in case there was anyone hiding in there. But both places were empty.

It looked as if Nolan actually had killed himself, she thought sadly, returning to his body. But why had he done it? What was his motive?

Despair?

Guilt?

Daria took out her handkerchief and used it to pick up the note by one of its corners. She laid it on the desk beside the lone lamp and read it quickly.

"'I did it. I killed that girl and dumped her body on Colton's ranch. I can't live with the guilt, so I am ending it and me. Nolan Sharpe.'"

The note was typed. She stared at the paper and read it again. And then a third time. The suicide note left a bad taste in her mouth.

Something was off, she thought.

Who typed a suicide note? Sharpe didn't strike her as the type who tried to be neat and tidy. If he had written the note, it should have been by hand, most likely illegible, she thought.

And what had he used to type it? she suddenly wondered, looking around the room. There was no laptop, no computer and no printer. Was this all premeditated? Had he gone to the library, which housed computers for people to use, and typed his suicide note there?

Had anyone seen him do it?

It just didn't hold together for her, but Daria had to report what she'd found to the sheriff. Maybe her superior would have a different take on this than she did. She knew he really was supposed to be hands-off when it came to this whole investigation, but she needed someone else's input. And Trey was by far the best lawman she knew, she thought, taking out her cell phone.

Pressing the first number on her contact list, she waited for him to pick up.

"Sheriff Colton," Trey said.

"Sheriff, it's Daria." She looked down at the dead man on the floor. "You're never going to believe what I just found."

When he began to speak, she realized that the sheriff sounded as if she'd just woken him up. "I've gone home for the night, Daria, and you should, too." She thought she heard him stifle a yawn. "Can this wait until morning?"

"I don't think so." She frowned, looking at the pool of blood next to Sharpe's left temple. "You're going to want to see this."

"Define 'this,'" Trey requested wearily. He had a feeling that sleep was just going to have to wait.

She took a deep breath then said, "I'm standing over Nolan Sharpe's dead body."

There was a pause on the other end of the line. "I take it that's not the beginning of a punch line," Trey said.

"Nope, afraid not."

"Where are you?" the sheriff asked. "I'll call the medical examiner and have him send someone out."

"At the Roaring Springs Motel. Room 212."

"What were you doing there?" Trey demanded. Holding his cell against his ear with his shoulder, he tucked in his shirt, then reached for his jacket. The temperature had dropped over twenty degrees and it promised to be an exceptionally cold night.

"Following up on another anonymous tip," she told him evasively. "The others all fell through or wound up leading nowhere."

Slipping on his jacket, he took his keys out to lock the front door. "And this one led you to a body?"

"A body with an interesting suicide note," she told him. "The guy said he couldn't take the guilt anymore and that was why he was killing himself."

Locking the door, Trey made his way to his vehicle. "Guilt about what?"

"According to the note, he was the one who killed that girl your cousin found on his property. Bianca Rouge," she added.

Getting in behind the wheel, Trey inserted the key into the ignition. "You don't sound convinced," he observed.

"I'm not."

Chapter 18

Trey arrived at the motel a few minutes after the medical examiner pulled up in front of it. It took the sheriff less than five minutes to ascertain that the ME was having a lot less difficulty in writing off the crime scene than Daria was.

"Looks like a cut-and-dried case of suicide to me," the man pronounced.

"Give us a few minutes to take pictures," Trey requested, handing the camera to Daria.

The medical examiner looked impatient but gestured for him to go ahead.

After taking in the entire scene and having taken the appropriate amount of photographs depicting the room, the surrounding area and the dead man, Trey stepped aside to give the ME space to remove the body.

"Finally," the disgruntled man mumbled. "Okay, bring it up," he called to his assistant, referring to the gurney.

Trey turned to his deputy.

"All right," he said to Daria, "tell me what's bothering you about this case."

"It didn't make sense," she admitted. "Something isn't adding up."

"Like what?" There was no impatience or judgment in his voice. He wanted to know.

"What did a two-bit inept thief have in common with a high-class, high-priced call girl?" she told him. "They just don't strike me as having traveled in the same circles. This guy wasn't even on the radar for something like this," she noted. "If it wasn't for that anonymous tip, I wouldn't have even looked twice at the man."

Trey shrugged. He saw her point; however, life was often stranger than fiction in his opinion. And there could be lots of explanations for what was bothering his deputy.

"Maybe she knew him from her past life. Maybe they're originally from the same neighborhood or they went to the same high school. You never know," he pointed out as they walked out of the room. "Besides, this gets Russ Colton and his demands to clear his son off our backs. No small thing. Not to mention," Trey continued, "that the state authorities are pressuring us to close the case. You did good, Daria," he told her.

"I did nothing," she contradicted, dismissing his praise. "I just walked in on a dead body."

"And closed the case," he stressed.

Maybe, she thought. *And maybe not.*

Trey could see that wasn't enough for her. He knew what it was like to have a case eating away at you.

"If it makes you feel any better," he told her, "look into both their backgrounds and see if you can find anything that might have put them together at any time in the past."

Trey's deputy nodded. She fully intended to do just that, even if she had to do it on her own time. But having Trey's blessing made things easier.

Trey lost no time in calling Wyatt later that morning and telling him about Nolan Sharpe's suicide note. "You're out of the woods. Looks like life can get back to being normal for you."

"Well, it's really good to hear that I'm not a suspect in this murder anymore, but my life is far from normal yet," Wyatt said to his cousin.

"What do you mean?"

"Aside from my bull being poisoned, two of my calves were found injured shortly after Brahma was poisoned, and a third calf, according to my men, just went missing." There was barely suppressed frustration evident in Wyatt's voice. "Someone is messing with my herd."

Trey remembered the last call he'd received from

his cousin. "You still think Everett Olson's behind it?" he asked.

"I do. I know he's got an alibi as far as my bull is concerned, but there isn't anyone else who stands to gain anything if I wind up losing most of my herd and going bankrupt." Wyatt exhaled sharply. "He's been trying to buy my land and he's not the type to take no for an answer."

Wyatt had a temper when provoked; Trey was well aware of that. "Don't do anything crazy," he warned.

Not that Wyatt hadn't been tempted, but he was also aware of the consequences that went along with any rash actions.

"And give him the satisfaction of seeing me arrested when he presses charges? Not on your life. That doesn't mean that I'm not going to find a way to get that no good son of a bitch to confess to what he's been up to."

"As long as you remember to do it by the book, Wyatt," Trey reminded him.

"Yeah, yeah, I know." Wyatt sighed. "Well, thanks for giving me the heads-up, Trey. Talk soon," he said just before terminating the call.

"What was that all about?" Bailey asked as she came down the stairs. She had walked in on the tail end of the conversation from Wyatt's side. And it had aroused her curiosity.

Wyatt turned around and saw her. "Morning, Sunshine. Feeling rested?" he asked. "You slept around the clock," he said, suppressing a grin.

She looked stunned for a moment then realized he was teasing her. "I did not," she protested.

"No, you didn't," he confessed, his grin surfacing. "But you have to admit this is rather late for you." She was usually up right around five, or at least that was what she'd been doing since she'd returned. "It's closer to nine than to eight. Those are real banker's hours," he teased.

"Only if the banker delivers calves and looks after injured ones," she replied, coming up to him.

"Good point." Drawing Bailey into his arms, Wyatt said, "Good news for a change. Trey just called and said they found the guy who killed that woman we found on our ranch."

He said "our" not "my," Bailey noticed. Was that just a careless slip of the tongue or did he actually mean it? Her heart fluttered in her chest. Did he think of the ranch as theirs now?

Don't get ahead of yourself, she warned. It could just be that he didn't know how to refer to the Crooked C since they had both owned it at one time.

Bailey forced herself to focus on the gist of what her ex-husband was telling her and not on what she *wanted* him to say.

"That's wonderful," she told Wyatt. Then two questions occurred to her. "How did they find him? Did they arrest him?"

"That wasn't necessary," he replied. When she silently raised a quizzical eyebrow, he explained. "He's dead."

She jumped to the only logical conclusion she could. "Did he try to escape and they shot him?"

"No," Wyatt answered. "According to Trey, the guy committed suicide because he felt so guilty about what he'd done."

"Well, he should have felt guilty," she said, angry. "He not only killed the girl, he deliberately tried to put the blame on you." She wove her arms around Wyatt's neck, focusing on the fact that this was a well-deserved win for him. She didn't have time to waste being furious with a dead man. "This is wonderful, Wyatt. You've got your life back."

Having her against him like this caused all sorts of things to spring to life within him. He smiled down into her face. "And I know just how to celebrate," he whispered, his breath fanning along her lips.

He was the only man who could ever get to her so quickly and completely. "Oh? How?" Bailey asked innocently.

If he gave in and kissed her, it wouldn't stop there. He knew that. He had to keep himself in check. Now wasn't the time to give in. But soon—

"I'll show you tonight," he promised, stroking a thumb against her cheek. "But right now, we have a full day of work ahead of us."

Bailey nodded. He was right. Tonight they'd have their privacy. At the moment they ran the risk of being interrupted if one of his men came pounding on the door, looking for him.

"Then we'd better get started," she said. Extricating herself from his arms, she started to head for the front door.

"Wait," Wyatt protested. "Don't you want to have breakfast first?" he asked.

"No, I'll eat later," she told him. "My stomach's feeling a bit queasy. Probably something I ate didn't agree with me," she added quickly.

Instantly alert, Wyatt immediately thought of his bull. No one had been able to figure out how Brahma had gotten the poison into his system. "You didn't eat anything unusual, did you?"

She saw the leery look in his eyes. "No. Why?"

He debated just waving this away, but he'd never be able to forgive himself if something happened to her because he hadn't explored every possibility. "Maybe I'm just being paranoid—" he prefaced his words "—but ever since Brahma was poisoned…"

She knew where Wyatt was going with this and stopped him before he could continue. "You're right," she said, returning to his side to give him a quick kiss. "You're being paranoid. But I think it's very sweet. And sometimes a stomachache is just a stomachache. Now let's go."

Maybe she was right, he thought. With a sigh, he surrendered.

For now.

It was a regular workday.

Some of the older calves had to be branded so that they couldn't be easily stolen, something Wyatt felt Olson would attempt next.

The paranoia he was experiencing didn't all stem from Olson and his poisoned bull. It actually went back further than that. There had been bad blood between Wyatt and the other rancher ever since the latter had tried to buy his ranch and was turned down. In a moment of unguarded hostility, Olson had promised that Wyatt would live to regret the day he had rejected his offer.

It was quite possible, Wyatt thought, that Olson was now trying to make his prophesy come true.

But there was too much work to get done for him to waste any time dwelling on a man he had come to actively hate.

What he did take note of, though, was that he saw Bailey working as hard as any of the hands. She didn't just keep to the barn, restricting herself to looking after the calves and the pregnant milk cows. She went anywhere there was work to be done.

The fence along the western perimeter needed replacing and Bailey was right there beside him, as handy with a hammer and planks of wood as any of his hired hands.

In Silas Jacobs's case, Wyatt thought with a smile, better.

"You're grinning like a kid who just won first prize at the county fair," Bailey pointed out as she finished up.

His eyes washed over her just for a second. "Maybe I did," he told her, a satisfied smile curving his mouth.

Bailey cocked her head, studying him. "Is that a compliment?" she asked. "I can't tell."

Wyatt winked. "Make of it what you will."

She knew what she wanted to make of it, but she also knew what could happen if she got ahead of herself and started to read more into the situation than what actually existed. She didn't want to be disappointed. Seeing compliments where none were intended was akin to trying to grab a runaway buzz saw with her bare hands. The outcome wound up being far too painful for words.

"I find that it's never a good idea to allow my imagination to just run away with me," she told Wyatt seriously.

He could understand that. He'd been there himself.

"I can respect that," he answered. He promised himself to do something about that tonight.

They worked until well after dark, ending up in the main barn. Bailey wanted to check on how the herd was doing before they called it a night. Despite precautions, today another one of the calves had gotten mysteriously hurt. The calf had somehow managed to get itself stuck on some of the barbed wire. It didn't seem possible, given where the wire was located and where the calf had been initially, but for now she didn't try to figure out how the calf had strayed that far and just focused on keeping the wounds from becoming infected.

The calf didn't feel like cooperating, and making sure the wounds were clean and bandaged took longer than anticipated.

"Mind if I take a rain check for that celebration you had in mind?" Bailey asked Wyatt when they finally made their way into the house. She felt so drained, she could barely put one foot in front of the other. Her lack of energy was a complete mystery to her.

"Consider it rain-checked," he told her. "I'll go fix us a late dinner. Should be something there I can work with," he added.

"I'm not hungry," she said, stopping him before he could go to the kitchen.

Turning, he shot her a concerned look. "You skipped breakfast," he reminded her and then realized something else. "You haven't eaten all day."

"And I'm still standing," Bailey managed to respond playfully.

He wasn't as amused by her comment as she was. "Yeah, but for how long?"

"Long enough to crawl into bed," Bailey told him. She walked over to the stairs.

He crossed to her, tilting her chin up to meet his eyes. "Bailey, you can't go on this way."

"And I won't," she promised. "But it doesn't hurt to occasionally go a day without eating. Some people do it deliberately on a regular basis. They schedule it," she told him.

He frowned, unconvinced. "And some people like

to jump out of airplanes… Doesn't mean everyone should do it."

She was not in the mood for a debate. "Now you're just reaching. I'm bone-tired and *not* hungry." Her tone changed. "Let me just crawl into bed, Wyatt. I promise I'll be more fun tomorrow."

"You were just great today," he told her, letting her know that being "more fun" wasn't necessary. "A complete partner," Wyatt added, his eyes pinning her in place for a moment.

She smiled, wondering if he realized how much of a compliment that was to her and what it meant to hear him say that.

Maybe if he'd said things like that when she'd been here the first time as his wife, she would have never felt motivated to go off on her own.

Still, Bailey silently argued with herself as she went up the stairs, if she hadn't left, she would have never become a veterinarian, and that was a very large part of who she was. Because she had become one had allowed her feelings of self-worth to go up 100 percent. And if she hadn't done all that, she wouldn't have been able to help his herd the way she had today.

That would have been a huge loss.

This was way too much for her to contemplate right now, Bailey decided. All she needed to think about was that her life was on the right track. She and Wyatt had at least a temporary truce in place, if not more. And, more important, if she was ever going to get pregnant, it had to be now and he had agreed to help her achieve her goal. That was the only thing that mattered.

That and the fact that Wyatt was no longer under suspicion of murder.

By the time Bailey's head hit the pillow, she was already asleep.

With a smile on her face.

The sound of raised voices echoed in her head, dissolving her dream bit by bit until Bailey was sitting up, listening, even though her brain was not totally engaged just yet.

Were those really raised voices or part of a dream she was having?

Getting out of bed, she grabbed her clothes and swiftly put them on as she tried to make out what was being said.

Shouting. She was hearing shouting, she realized. Angry shouting.

What the hell was going on?

She looked out the window and was stunned to see there had to be at least a dozen people, if not more, gathered in front of the house. It seemed like all of them were bellowing for Wyatt to come out and face them instead of hiding in the house "like a coward."

Incensed, she ran out of the bedroom and flew down the stairs, instinctively knowing that at any second now Wyatt would go out there to face down the mob. And they were in such a volatile mood, there was no telling how they would react if they saw him.

She had to get to him before he went out.

Reaching the bottom of the stairs, she saw Wyatt. He looked angry and had one hand on the doorknob.

Fear spiked through her, twisting in her chest like a sharp knife.

"Wyatt, no!"

Chapter 19

"We know you did it, Colton!" someone in the mob shouted. "You're the one who kidnapped Cynthia Gates! Did you kill her, too?"

Another man, standing at the rear of the mob, hollered, "Your daddy might have gotten you off the first time, but he's not gonna be able to do it a second time! You're gonna rot in a prison cell if they don't execute you for this first!"

A third voice joined the others. "Come out and show yourself, you damn coward!"

"Prison's too good for him!" someone else shouted, agitating the mob even further.

The look on Wyatt's face told Bailey that he was going out to face these people, but given how incensed they were, she was really afraid for his safety.

Bailey threw herself in front of the door, pressing her back against it as she turned to face Wyatt just as he was about to reach for the doorknob a second time.

"You can't go out there, Wyatt," she cried.

"Well, I'm not about to hide from them in here," he told her.

Putting his hands on her shoulders, he tried to move her aside, but she was surprisingly strong as she held fast, refusing to budge.

"Wyatt, be reasonable," she pleaded. "You *can't* go out there. They'll tear you to pieces—and not figuratively," she emphasized. "Call the sheriff. Call somebody that hasn't been worked up into a frenzy," she implored him. "Somebody has to get control over this mob before they do something really terrible that can't be undone."

Wyatt shook his head. "Nobody's going to get here in time to do anything," he said, dismissing her idea. He saw that Bailey had pulled out her cell and she looked as if she was going to call someone.

He could take care of this mob himself, he thought angrily. "Put that thing away, Bailey," he ordered.

But she wasn't about to be intimidated and back off. "I'm calling Fox and telling him to get the ranch hands." His ranch was carved out of Wyatt's property and he was close enough to be able to get here fast. "They can help hold these people in check before Trey and his deputies get here."

Wyatt sighed indignantly then waved her on. "All right, go ahead," he told her between gritted teeth.

Her eyes narrowed as she shot Wyatt a dark look. "I wasn't asking for permission."

The phone on the other end rang three times before she finally heard it being picked up. "Fox?" she cried, doing her best not to sound as desperate as she felt.

"Who's this?" the deep voice asked. Fox was obviously distracted. It sounded as if she'd gotten him in the middle of something.

Bailey had no time to offer any apologies. "Fox, it's Bailey. There's a bunch of people from town in front of Wyatt's door and they're demanding that he come out. They're shouting something about a missing woman. We don't know what's going on, but it looks like we need to even up the numbers a little before something awful happens. Can you—?"

She didn't need to finish her sentence. "I'll be right over," Fox promised. "Tell Wyatt to hang in there!" he instructed just before terminating the call.

"We're definitely going to try," she said into the now silent phone. She began pressing numbers again.

"*Now* who are you calling?" Wyatt wanted to know.

The mob standing outside his door sounded as if it was growing even more unruly. The shouting had become louder and even more frenzied.

"The sheriff," Bailey answered. "I'm going to— Sheriff Colton?" she said, immediately alert and turning her attention to the person who had just picked up on the other end.

"Hello? Bailey?" Trey asked. "Is that you? What's up?"

"Yes, it's me." Her number must have popped up on his screen. "Something awful's about to happen. I think you should know that there's a big crowd of people in front of Wyatt's house and it sounds like they are getting really surly. Wyatt said you told him yesterday that someone else had confessed to killing Bianca, so is there something going on that we don't know about?"

"Damn," she heard Trey mutter.

"That doesn't explain anything, Sheriff," she told him, even though his reaction confirmed her suspicions. Something *was* going on.

The next moment the phone was yanked out of her hand as Wyatt got on it.

"Trey, this is Wyatt. Why the hell is there an angry mob gathered in front of my place shouting for my blood?"

"Cynthia Gates has gone missing. Some people think you're to blame. We'll talk when I get there. Keep your doors locked!" Trey ordered. "I'll be there as fast as I can—with backup."

"Backup?" Wyatt repeated, stunned at how out of hand this was getting. "This is beginning to sound like an episode out of some cop show on TV," he complained.

"Remember, whatever you do, *don't open the door*. I'll get to you as fast as I can," Trey promised.

The line went dead.

"So what's going on?" Bailey demanded, searching Wyatt's face for some sort of a sign that he knew. "Did he tell you?"

He didn't want to alarm her, so he pretended not to know. "I have no idea," Wyatt said. "You heard me just ask Trey. He said he'd get to me as fast as he could and then ended the call."

"Hey, Colton, you gotta come out sometime. You can't hide in there forever and we're prepared to wait you out! We can stay out here all day if we have to!" someone at the head of the mob promised.

Bailey saw the vein in Wyatt's neck stand out, throbbing. She knew what was happening. Wyatt was trying to contain himself, but just the opposite was happening. He was working himself up. He'd always hated not confronting things head-on, but this time, if he did that, she was really afraid that something awful was going to happen to him.

Only a show of force would be able to get this angry, out-of-control mob to calm down. And no matter how indignant Wyatt was, he was only one man and he didn't represent the law the way that Trey and his people did. If he went out now, the mob would wind up rushing him.

Them, she amended, because she wasn't about to allow Wyatt to possibly be dragged off without trying to hold the mob off herself.

"Wyatt," she cautioned, "you open that door and I go out with you."

"No, you won't," he contradicted, his voice more stern and foreboding than she'd ever heard it sounding. "You'll lock the door right behind me and stay inside no matter what you hear or see."

She stood there with her legs spread apart, stable and unshakable, staring him down.

"The hell I will, Wyatt. And I mean it," she snapped angrily. "You go out, I go out. Or," she said, giving him an alternative, "we wait here until Fox, the sheriff and their people get here." She watched the vein in his neck throb. He didn't want to agree. "For once in your life, use your head!"

He looked at her, his expression a mixture of surprise and anger. "What did you just say?"

There was a time when that look on his face would have silenced her. But that time was over. She wasn't about to back down. This was too important.

"You heard me," she told him. "We've just started to regain ground and rebuild something. I am *not* about to watch you being torn limb from limb right in front of me because you're too pigheaded and stupid to stay inside the house where you're safe—"

Bailey jumped, stifling a scream as someone threw a rock through one of the windows.

"Or relatively so," she amended, her heart pounding wildly in response to the breaking glass and the rock that landed close to her feet.

"Back off out there!" Wyatt shouted.

He would have gone to the window but Bailey grabbed hold of his arm and held him back as hard as she could. She had no doubt that if she hadn't, he would have torn out the door—straight into the mob.

"That rock some idiot just threw almost hit my wife," he shouted, his voice carrying through the broken window.

"Then come out, coward! We want you, not her!" someone in the mob shouted.

It sounded like the first man who had yelled earlier. Wyatt had a feeling he was the ringleader—or at least one of them.

"If you don't come out, we're coming in!" someone else threatened. His voice was beginning to become familiar, too. "No telling how things'll go then, coward!" the man sneered.

That did it. A man could only put up with so much before reacting. Wyatt spun on his heel and headed to the den. Less than two minutes later, he was back in the living room, carrying his rifle and a box of shells. He saw the look in Bailey's eyes and guessed what she was probably thinking. He wasn't about to walk out, gun blazing.

"Last resort," he told her.

But that wasn't what she was going to ask him. "Where's mine?"

The smile on his lips was grim. "Back in the den, but maybe you shouldn't—"

She'd already left the room. She was not about to stand still and listen to him lecture her when their safety was being threatened.

"I'm a better shot than you are," she informed him, raising her voice to be heard above the ever-growing din outside. "If they rush us, we'll shoot over their heads, maybe scare them enough to back off."

The sound of a rifle being discharged several times froze her in her tracks. She looked quizzically at Wyatt. He hadn't fired, but someone in the mob obviously had. Was this it? Was the mob about to storm into the ranch house? She ran for the den to retrieve another weapon.

Three more shots were discharged as she ran back in, followed by a voice they both recognized.

"Everybody take a deep breath and count to ten. Or, if that's too hard for you, as high as you can go without straining your brains. Now, everybody take a step back!"

"Fox!" she cried. Her relief turned to fear as she saw Wyatt open the door. "Wyatt, wait! Don't!"

But it was too late. Wyatt had already opened the front door and was stepping out onto the porch, his rifle held ready in his hands.

He smiled when he saw his brother.

Fox hadn't come alone.

"Damn but it's good to see your ugly mug," Wyatt said. He wasn't looking at Fox but at one of the men Fox had brought with him.

Liam Kastor, tall, blond and solid muscle, was his best friend as well as a detective with the Roaring Springs Police Department.

Fox, standing at the back of the mob, nodded in

response to Wyatt's acknowledgment. "He'd just dropped by my place to see about buying one of my horses when Bailey called me. I didn't think you'd mind if I brought him along."

"Can all the talk!" a deep voice from the center of the mob snarled. "We're here to drag Colton's murdering butt back to town to face the consequences of what he's done!"

It was obvious that Fox had more patience than Wyatt did, but it was not an endless supply and the mob had a way of eroding it.

Before he could say something in response, Liam, representing the law's side, spoke up. "McNutley, they found the guy who killed that prostitute," he informed the hotheaded man. Liam had his service revolver in his hand and it was trained on McNutley the second he'd started shouting.

"Or so you say," another man in the mob jeered. "Heard he conveniently killed himself so we wouldn't hear his side of the story. Colton's daddy probably paid to have that guy framed as the killer!"

Several others added their voices, agreeing.

"We don't have a quarrel with anyone else here," another one of the men said to Liam. "Just give yourself up, Wyatt, and we'll bring you in. You need to confess what you did with Cynthia!"

Despite the ring of ranch hands standing with Fox and the detective, it looked as if the mob had made up its mind to surge toward the house and grab Wyatt.

Never taking his eyes off the mob, Wyatt instinctively pushed Bailey behind him.

"Get back in the house," he ordered her sternly.

For just a split second her head spun and Bailey suddenly felt as if she was going to pass out. Somehow she managed to hang on, telling herself whatever this odd feeling was, it would pass. She was not about to leave Wyatt's side and this was no time to faint like some damsel in distress.

"No!"

She thought she shouted the word, but from the expression on Wyatt's face, she realized she had barely whispered it. She doubled down, grasping strength from somewhere.

"Bailey?" Wyatt asked, concerned about her despite the situation he was in.

"I don't remember deputizing any of you," a deep voice said, addressing the back end of the mob.

Hearing the cavernous, steady voice, Bailey could have wept with sheer relief.

The mob turned almost in unison to look behind them and saw that Trey, Daria and several deputies from the local police department were positioned strategically behind them. A couple, including the sheriff, were standing on the flatbed of a truck, towering over the mob.

All were armed and all had their weapons pointed at the people comprising the mob.

"Now, if you all know what's good for you," Trey continued as if he was talking to a single person, "you'll just disperse and head on back to your shops and homes. You do that and we'll forget this ever happened."

It wasn't going to be that easy.

"He kidnapped another one, Sheriff," McNutley said angrily. "For all you know, he's got her tied up in his house or the barn. Or maybe he killed her like that other one and she's lying somewhere where the coyotes can get at her so you won't be able to recognize her when you do find her," McNutley shouted, drawing a gruesome scenario for everyone.

It sparked another angry reaction that was about to turn ugly.

Trey held up his hand, quieting the crowd. He shook his head. "That's some imagination you have there, Boyd," he told McNutley. "You should be putting it to better use and writing fiction for a living instead of stirring up a crowd." Looking over his shoulder, he suddenly called out to one of his deputies. "Hey, Alejandro, why don't you bring our guest over here so everyone can get a good look at her?"

Disgruntled voices talked over one another as people within the tight mob speculated about what was going on.

"I believe everyone's looking for you, Cynthia," Trey said to the young woman Alejandro brought out from his vehicle. "From what they just said, some of them are sure you're dead." He held his hand out to have her join him on the truck's flatbed. "Why don't you tell them where you were?" he coaxed. The smile on his lips was only paper-thin.

When the girl said nothing, Trey merely nodded as if he hadn't really expected anything from her.

"Cynthia here decided to run off and spend 'forever' with the love of her life, but apparently 'the love of her life' didn't have anything long-term in mind. Forever turned out to have a very short life span and one of my deputies found her about twenty miles out of town, drunk and disoriented, but most definitely alive." He turned and his eyes swept over the crowd. "And Wyatt Colton never touched her, never even knew who she was," he informed the members of the mob.

Trey scowled at various faces within the crowd. His voice was still low and even, but there was no mistaking the barely contained wrath that was there just beneath. "You were going to make an innocent man pay for something he didn't do just because you don't like his father. Think about that the next time you want to rush off and dispense 'justice,'" he reprimanded them angrily. "And after you finish thinking, do yourselves—and me—a favor and *stay the hell put.*"

Chapter 20

Robbed of their fire and no longer able to wrap themselves up in righteous indignation, the participants of the mob moved as one and parted, allowing the sheriff to walk up to Wyatt.

Before saying a word, Trey looked at the broken window then turned to his cousin. "You want to press charges against anybody, Wyatt?" he asked, waving his hand at the men in the front of the crowd.

Wyatt shook his head. "Not yet," he answered. "I need to better assess how much damage they actually did to my ranch. For now, I just want this to be over." His eyes swept across some of the faces of the men at the front of the group. "That means get off my land!" he ordered angrily.

"You heard the man," Trey said, addressing the

people in the crowd who had, for the most part, settled down. "Leave before I decide to have you all
arrested for trespassing!"

That was all the group needed to hear. Some still
grumbling, the people comprising the crowd dis-
persed and went to their vehicles. Getting in, they
left the premises as quickly as possible.

Satisfied that the danger—at least for now—was
over, Trey turned to Daria, who had been beside him
since they had arrived.

"Take Cynthia back to her parents," he instructed.
He looked at the runaway who had indirectly been
responsible for stirring up this particular hornet's
nest. "Once they stop hugging her, I'm sure they'll
have a few words to share with this young lady about
her behavior."

Taking the young woman's arm, Daria started to
escort Cynthia to her police vehicle. "You got it,
Sheriff," the deputy said.

Fox, Liam and Trey hung back, remaining near
Wyatt and Bailey as the last of the crowd broke up
under the watchful eyes of the deputies and the ranch
hands who had all come to Wyatt's aid.

"You going to be all right?" Fox wanted to know,
looking from Wyatt to Bailey.

"We'll be fine now," Wyatt assured him. "Thanks
to all of you," he added, his gaze taking in his friends
and the ranch hands.

"Hey, don't thank us," Fox told him. "Thank Bailey." When his eyes met hers, Bailey's face flushed.

"We wouldn't have gotten here in time if she hadn't called."

"Oh, yeah, I forgot about that." With everything happening at once and fearing for Bailey's safety, he'd lost track of the order that everything had unfolded. A crooked smile lifted the corners of Wyatt's mouth as he turned to his ex-wife. She was looking rather pale again, he thought. "Are you feeling all right?" he asked. "You want to go in and lie down?"

Bailey waved away his concern. "I'm fine," she insisted, even though her stomach felt like a small ship riding out a particularly choppy wave.

Wyatt nodded, going with the gist of her words instead of her ghostly complexion. "If you say so." Then he turned toward the men who had all come to lend their support. "Why don't we all meet up downtown come Saturday and I'll buy you all a couple of rounds of drinks," he offered, adding, "Just my way of saying thanks."

"Don't have to twist my arm," Fox replied with a laugh.

"I'll take you up on that, as well," Liam said, adding his voice to Fox's.

"You can count me in, too," Trey said, "once I make sure that Daria's covering for me." He shifted his weight, his eyes washing over Wyatt. "But now that the home front's safe, I've got to be getting back."

"I've got calves to look after." Bailey spoke up, excusing herself.

Wyatt knew that he had more than enough work to see to, as well. The angry mob had temporarily made him forget about that. "What she said," he added, pointing his finger at Bailey.

With the threat to Wyatt and the ranch over, at least for now, the remainder of the group all went their separate ways.

It was only after the sheriff had left with his deputies that Murphy approached Wyatt. "Boss," he called to Wyatt.

The latter stopped in his tracks, giving his foreman an inquisitive look. "Something on your mind?"

Murphy nodded. "I think you might want to hear something."

Now what? Wyatt wondered, sparing Bailey a glance. She seemed as much in the dark as he was.

"What is it?" Wyatt asked.

"I was talking to my friend Billy last night." Murphy paused. "Ever since his wife took ill and died on him, he doesn't like coming home to an empty house," the foreman explained, "so most nights, he stops off at the bar downtown."

"Is this going somewhere?" he asked, doing his best not to sound impatient.

The mob had put him behind schedule and he wanted to get back to work as soon as possible. He was certain there were probably a lot of breaks in the fencing to repair, thanks to the townspeople's impromptu visit.

Murphy nodded. "According to him, Olson wasn't at the bar the night he said he was."

Wyatt became alert. "Is this friend of yours sure?" he pressed.

"If he was drinking—" Bailey interjected, a skeptical look on her face.

"Billy doesn't get drunk. He just sits and nurses one beer for as long as he can before finally going home. And he's sure," Murphy answered, looking at Wyatt.

Bailey grew excited. "That means that Olson paid the bartender to back up his lie," she cried.

"Sure looks that way," Wyatt agreed. He looked at his foreman. "Can you handle things around here? I'm going into town to verify this with the bartender, and if his story holds up—and Olson's lie doesn't—I'm going to go pay Mr. Olson a little visit." His expression grew steely. "See if maybe I can jog his memory about the evening in question."

"Sure thing, boss." Murphy grinned just before heading to the barn. "Lucky thing I talked to Billy," he said, pleased at how things had turned out.

"Very lucky," Wyatt agreed as he hurried off to his truck.

Someone had broken his windshield, he noted as he approached the vehicle. Had to be the mob. It looked like maybe he would be pressing charges after all, he thought grimly.

It wasn't until he started to get into the truck's cab that he saw Bailey had followed him and was on the other side of the truck, opening the passenger door. He scowled. "Where do you think you're going?"

"With you, of course," she answered, getting in.

Where the hell had she gotten that impression? "No, you're not. You're staying here," he ordered.

There was a trace of exasperation in Bailey's eyes as she looked at him. "You haven't learned yet, have you, Wyatt?" she asked. "I don't take orders from you."

He was not in the mood for a heated debate. "Look, the man poisoned my bull and he's undoubtedly responsible for hurting my calves."

Was that supposed to get her to stay on the ranch? Didn't he know her by now? "All the more reason for me to come with you."

Talk about being thickheaded, Wyatt thought, suppressing an annoyed sigh. Nothing was ever easy with this woman.

"He's *dangerous*, Bailey."

The smile began in her eyes as she assured him, "And so am I. Start the truck, Wyatt."

He put the key in the ignition. "I don't want you getting hurt."

"And I don't want *you* getting hurt," she countered in the same tone, mimicking him. "So we're agreed. We'll have each other's backs so neither one of us will get hurt dealing with this worthless scum."

There were times like these when he could have strangled her. But since there was no convincing her and they were wasting time, he had no choice but to let her come along. Wyatt turned the key, starting the truck. He shot an irritated glance in her direction. "You can still drive me crazy faster than anyone else I know," he told her.

Bailey merely took his comment in stride as she settled in. "Right back at you, Wyatt," she responded.

They rode into the town's downtown area. At this hour of the morning it was fairly empty and he had his pick of parking spots. Pulling his truck close to the squat one-story building deliberately built to resemble a log cabin, Wyatt got out.

"You can stay here. No need for both of us to go in," he told her.

Nonetheless, Bailey got out. "Nice try," she told him. "I'm coming with you."

They walked into the darkened establishment. Only half the lights were on.

"We're not open yet," the bartender called out from the far end of the bar.

"We're not here to drink," Wyatt told the thin, bald man polishing the bar.

"You need to leave. This isn't a gathering place," Ned Peters told them.

By then Wyatt had crossed the room and was at the bar, looking at the bartender. The man was of average height and sporting the beginnings of a beard to make up for the fact that he was losing his hair.

"What do you want?" Peters snapped. "I can call the sheriff."

"Go ahead, Peters," Wyatt told him. "Then you can tell him why you lied to him."

"What are you talking about?" the man demanded, substituting bravado for his dwindling courage.

"You told the sheriff that Olson was here the night that Wyatt's bull was poisoned," Bailey said, unable to keep quiet any longer.

Peters drew himself up as if standing more erect would somehow negate his lie. "He was."

"No, he wasn't," Wyatt retorted. "One of your regulars was here that night and he said he didn't see Olson here," he informed the bartender, towering over the man.

Peters took a step back, despite the fact that the bar was between them. His fearful eyes never left Wyatt's face. "He made a mistake."

"Or you did," Wyatt countered sternly. "How much did Olson pay you to lie for him?"

Perspiration began to appear on the bartender's forehead. "I—"

"How much?" Wyatt demanded, his face darkening as his eyes pinned Peters in place.

"It'll go easier on you if you tell him the truth," Bailey told the bartender. "He doesn't react well to people lying to him."

Afraid, looking very much like a man who was cornered, Peters started to stutter. "I—I had all these… these debts. If I didn't pay up, I'd…I'd lose the bar."

"So you sold out instead," Wyatt concluded. It wasn't a guess.

"It was nothing personal," Peters babbled. "But this bar is all I have. You don't know what it's like to struggle all your life and face losing *everything* just when you finally thought you had a foothold in this world."

Wyatt merely looked at the other man coldly. "You don't know anything about me," he answered. "You're going to tell the sheriff the truth about this—that you lied for Olson."

"But Olson'll kill me if I tell," Peters cried.

"Confession is good for the soul," Wyatt responded. "And I'll kill you if you don't."

Peters caved.

"What the hell are you doing on my property?" Olson demanded as he answered the knock on his door. Seeing Wyatt and Bailey on his doorstep was not a welcome sight, especially when Wyatt pushed the door farther open so that he and Bailey could enter.

And then a smile that would have made a rattlesnake's heart turn to stone crossed the rancher's face as he regarded Wyatt.

"You reconsider selling?" he quipped.

"No," Wyatt answered. "I'm giving you a chance to give yourself up."

Olson's expression went from furious to mocking. "Oh, that's rich. And why, in your twisted logic, would I do that?"

"Because your story about where you were the

night Wyatt's bull was poisoned just fell apart," Bailey informed him.

Olson's face grew even darker and more foreboding as he glared at Bailey. "What are you talking about?" the rancher demanded.

"Your alibi fell apart," Wyatt told him. "The bartender grew a conscience and recanted."

The word meant nothing to Olson. "What the hell's that supposed to mean?" he retorted.

Wyatt's voice was eerily calm as he answered the question. "It means you're going to jail for poisoning my bull and for trying to destroy my herd."

The other man's face turned red. "You can't prove anything!" Olson yelled then began viciously cursing at him.

Unfazed, Wyatt told the other rancher, "Oh, yes, I can. Bailey and I had a nice little talk with Peters about your so-called alibi and he realizes that he was mistaken about the time and date. You were never in his place at all that day." Wyatt stepped closer to Olson, his manner fierce and intimidating. "I bet if we talk to your men one by one, one of them will confess to doing your dirty work for you to my calves. Maybe one of them even got you that poison you used to kill Brahma."

It was obvious that Olson was trying not to look nervous. "You're just bluffing," he accused.

Wyatt looked at the rancher coldly. "I wouldn't risk my freedom on that hope if I were you." He turned to Bailey. "Bailey, why don't you let the sheriff in so we can show Olson here just how much we're not bluffing?"

Olson reacted like a cornered animal. "You son of a bitch!" he cried, taking a swing at Wyatt. He missed.

Wyatt spun around and grabbed the larger man by his shirt, pushing him against a wall. It took everything he had to refrain from pummeling the rancher.

"I'd watch my mouth if I were you," he warned.

Although Olson was bigger than Wyatt, like most cowards, when someone stood up to them, the rancher backed off, afraid of the consequences if he challenged the angry man.

"Hey, easy. No need to go flying off the handle like that, Colton. We're all reasonable, law-abiding men here," Olson cried, clearly afraid of what Wyatt was liable to do next.

"Law abiding? Is that what you call it?" Wyatt demanded, incensed. "Poisoning my prizewinning bull when you couldn't get me to sell him to you is your idea of 'law abiding'?" he shouted at the man.

Olson really looked worried now. Worried and terrified.

"You said the sheriff was outside," he reminded Wyatt. "You do anything to me and it's you he'll be arresting—remember that!"

"Are you threatening me now?" Wyatt asked Olson in disbelief.

"Wyatt, don't let him goad you into doing something you'll regret," Bailey cautioned, worried that

Olson might make him snap. "If this gets complicated, you might not wind up getting the results you want." Not waiting for Wyatt to respond, she opened the door quickly. "I'd get in here now if I were you, Trey," she called to the sheriff.

Trey walked in and Olson immediately began babbling. "I don't know what this damn fool is raving about, Sheriff, but he's lying. I never—"

"Save it, Olson," Trey ordered. "Peters confessed that you paid him to lie about where you were the night Wyatt's bull was poisoned."

Olson began to breathe heavily. The rancher had the look of a desperate man now. "Doesn't prove anything," he protested.

"Nobody pays someone to provide them with an alibi unless they've got something to hide, Olson," Trey said in his calm voice. "And before you start racking that brain of yours to come up with some kind of a plausible excuse, someone else came forward, saying that they saw you on Wyatt's property the night that his bull was poisoned."

"I was just coming to make Colton another offer," Olson cried, sweating profusely now.

"So why didn't you make it?" Wyatt challenged.

"'Cause I decided I didn't want to see your high-handed, superior smug face, so I went home," Olson answered.

"No," Bailey contradicted, getting into the rancher's face. "You slinked home after poisoning that fine specimen of a bull." She was growing angrier by the minute. "You're nothing but a low-life coward, poisoning defenseless animals because you couldn't get your way to take over Wyatt's land. Well, guess what?" She was shouting into the rancher's face now. "You're *not* getting your way and you're going to pay for what you did to that bull and to those calves you lured away and injured." Finished, she glared at him.

"Why, you little bitch!" Olson snarled, lunging forward.

The next thing anyone knew, Wyatt had swung his fist right into Olson's nose. Hearing the rancher curse at Bailey had pushed him over the edge.

Olson howled and stumbled backward as he grabbed his nose, covering it. He howled again from the pain.

"He broke my nose!" he cried to Trey. "You saw that! Colton broke my nose for no reason. I want to press charges."

Trey took out his handcuffs. But instead of using them on Wyatt, he cuffed Olson's hands behind his back.

"Sorry, I blinked," he told Olson. "Must have missed it."

"You saw it!" Olson cried, looking at Bailey for backup.

She looked at him, the picture of innocence even though she would have loved to pummel the man herself. "All I saw was you bumping up against the door. That must be when you hit your nose," Bailey told the rancher in a completely innocent, serious voice.

"You're going to be sorry!" Olson cried. "All of you are going to be sorry."

Trey took hold of the rancher's arm and roughly steered him outside. "Now, you know better than to threaten a sheriff, Olson. Nothing good can ever come of that."

Olson went to Trey's vehicle unwillingly, howling and cursing.

"Once I get him settled into his new accommodations, why don't you come on down to press charges against Olson?"

"Sounds good to me," Wyatt answered. Turning to Bailey, he put his arm around her shoulders. "C'mon, I've got to get you home."

Chapter 21

"We didn't need to come back home, Wyatt. I want to go in with you when you press charges against that awful man," Bailey said, following Wyatt through the house as he paused only long enough to change his shirt before going out again.

"Bailey, no," he responded, turning around to face her. He quickly finished buttoning his shirt and then tucked it into his waistband. "I want you to stay home, understand?"

Bailey blew out an angry breath. They finally had proof that Olson had been behind all the things that had been going wrong on the ranch. The poisoning and the missing, injured calves were all thanks to Olson's doing. Wyatt was chomping at the bit to finally be able to press charges against the man who had been lusting after his property these last few months. She understood that. But what she didn't understand was why he was so dead-set against her accompanying him to the police station.

"Why can't I come with you?" Bailey wanted to know. She felt like they'd had this conversation before—his wanting her to stay safely cloistered out of harm's way—not once but several times. She had fought him each time—and won.

So why did he want to go through all this again?

Wyatt bracketed her shoulders, attempting to keep her in place symbolically if not in reality. "Because I'm worried about you." His eyes washed over her again. She still looked pale to him. "You really haven't been looking well the last few days."

The observation did not go over well. Bailey attempted to shrug him off.

"Just what every woman loves to hear," she quipped sarcastically. "You certainly have a silver tongue."

He held her in place a second time, trying to get his point across. "Bailey, I'm serious."

She frowned at him but this time she didn't shrug him off. "Even better."

"Bailey, I want you to get some rest, understand?" Wyatt slipped his arms around her, not to anchor her but to offer his comfort and support. "You've been working too hard and not getting enough rest. I appreciate all of it," he told her with sincerity. "But you're not going to do me any good, *Doctor* Norton, if you get sick, so think of this as taking preventative measures." He kissed her cheek. "Now get into bed and get some rest. I'll be back before you know it."

"Am I allowed to watch you go?" she asked.

There was still a touch of sarcasm in her voice, but he pretended to ignore it. "Sure. Just make sure you go to bed right after I leave," he replied.

Bailey grimaced but didn't challenge him as she walked outside and watched Wyatt head over to his truck.

Once inside his truck, he waved at her. She nodded her head then turned away and walked back into the ranch house. She heard the truck start up and drive away as she closed the door. She didn't like being left out or left behind.

She *definitely* wasn't in the mood to lie down and wait until Wyatt returned. Restless, Bailey crossed from the front of the house to the back. Opening the back door, she went out.

There was a small pond located just behind the house. The pond had attracted a number of ducks. There seemed to be a small community of them, aimlessly floating. Since Wyatt had pointed them out to her, she'd found that going out to watch them was a very peaceful, calming experience. But right now, seeing them milling about just added to her restless frustration.

She knew that Wyatt meant well. He wasn't trying to shut her out; he was trying to look out for her. But she didn't need looking after.

Yes, it was nice to know that he cared enough to

be worried about her health, but she was fine. Whatever she'd felt before was gone now and, besides, she wasn't made of glass. She didn't need coddling or to be treated as if she should be wrapped in tissue paper. Treating her as if she was helpless just made her want to prove she was anything *but* that.

No, damn it, Bailey told herself, spinning around on her heel and marching back into the house. She wasn't just going to stay home like an obedient little lapdog. She was going into town, to the sheriff's office.

Whether Wyatt was willing to admit it or not, he needed her there, she thought fiercely.

More likely than not, the press had probably caught a whiff of what was going on and was going to have a field day, putting their own spin on things. Maybe even casting more doubt on him again. Since she had returned to Roaring Springs, if she wasn't there with Wyatt when he came to press charges against Olson, the press would probably misinterpret that.

One photograph was still worth a thousand words, and if it was a photograph of Wyatt alone, those thousand words would no doubt be all wrong.

She *needed* to be there with him.

Bailey walked out of the ranch house and headed toward the garage. Out of the corner of her eye, she saw Murphy, who reached her vehicle just as Bailey was about to back up and drive off. Coming over to the driver's side, he motioned for her to roll down her window.

Had Wyatt told his foreman to make sure she didn't leave the ranch? she wondered.

No, she was being paranoid, Bailey told herself. Wyatt wouldn't do that. He wouldn't try to force her to stay put. Maybe there was something else that was wrong.

When she pressed the button and the driver's-side window went down, Murphy asked, "Doc Bailey, where're you headed?"

"I'm going into town, Murphy," she answered, watching his face and trying to gauge the foreman's reaction. "I don't want Wyatt facing the press all alone."

"He won't be alone, Doc," Murphy assured her. "The sheriff's gonna be there with him. Nothing to worry about."

Bailey shook her head. Murphy was sweet, she thought. But he was a man and men had a tendency to miss the important little details because they were always so busy looking at and fixating on what they considered to be the bigger picture.

"It's not the same thing, Murphy," she told him.

Clearly realizing he couldn't stop her, Murphy tried another approach. "I can drive you into town, Doc," the foreman offered.

Bailey smiled up at him, knowing that Murphy meant well and was only doing what he probably thought that Wyatt would want him to. But she didn't want to be treated as if she were helpless by the foreman, either.

"I've been driving long before I ever had an official license, Murphy."

There were times her father had been far too drunk to take the wheel when they were following the rodeo circuit. When that happened, it had been up to her to get them to where they'd needed to be. Being that young, she'd never once thought of the consequences if she was ever pulled over. She just drove.

It planted the seeds of fearlessness in her that was still there today.

Finally getting the hint that there was nothing he could do to stop her, the foreman nodded and stepped aside.

"Don't look so worried," she told Murphy. "I'll be fine."

"I hope so," he murmured.

The drive from the Crooked C to Roaring Springs was not a particularly long one, but it was definitely a winding one. Since there were no other cars or trucks on the road, she basked in the quiet solitude as she traveled through a beautiful yet lonely stretch of land.

As she drove, Bailey thought about what she was going to say to Wyatt when he saw her. She already knew he wasn't exactly going to be thrilled to see her—but she'd get him to understand why she *had* to be there.

Bailey smiled to herself, confident she was doing the right thing.

When she heard the sound of another car, she automatically looked in her rearview mirror since there was nothing in front of her except open space.

Bailey saw what looked like a sedan in the distance.

The car appeared to be catching up to her and showed no signs of slowing.

Where was this guy going in such a hurry? she wondered.

And why was he practically tailgating her? He had the entire open road in front of him. He could easily pass her and drive fast to his heart's content. It was rather idiotic to do that, she thought, but he could if he wanted to.

Bailey frowned. The man was clearly a jerk but she wasn't about to test how far his stupidity went. Instead she switched lanes, moving to the right and waving for the driver to pass her.

He didn't.

To her surprise, the driver of the black sedan switched lanes right along with her, getting right behind her again.

"What's wrong with you?" she cried out loud, even though she knew he couldn't hear her.

Okay, maybe the jerk just liked the right lane, she thought. Wanting to get away from him, Bailey switched lanes again, this time moving to the left lane.

And so did he.

Something was wrong, Bailey thought. She grew a little uneasy. Holding her breath and watching the driver in her rearview mirror, she switched lanes again. The driver was all but on top of her and he switched lanes right along with her.

There was hardly any space between the two vehicles now.

Bailey sped up again, pressing down on the gas pedal as hard as she could. She watched her speedometer inching up to seventy then seventy-five.

It continued climbing.

Her mouth felt dry enough to house cotton. This wasn't making any sense.

Was he trying to kill her?

The second the thought occurred to her, Bailey realized that as unbelievable as it sounded to her brain, she was right. Whoever was in that sedan was out to kill her.

Though it wasn't easy, Bailey forced herself to stop looking back. Instead she just focused on the road ahead. At these speeds, the curves were really dangerous, and if she wasn't careful, she could wind up going down the incline and crashing.

Bailey grasped the wheel tightly and tried to get ahead of the sedan.

When she felt the first jolt, she thought she had run something over. But the second, even harder jolt made her realize that the sedan that had been following her had hit her and was attempting to force her off the road.

She swerved into the next lane, but the road ahead narrowed and the two lanes merged, becoming just one. Bailey knew she had nowhere to go to avoid being rammed.

He did it again.

With her heart in her throat, Bailey pressed down on the accelerator as hard as she could while still desperately struggling to retain control over her swerving vehicle.

The sedan behind her sped up and rammed into her again.

This time the contact was so hard she could almost feel her teeth rattle. Although she was gripping the wheel so tightly that her fingers felt as if they were about to snap off, she did her best to maintain control of the vehicle and tried to maneuver the car away from the man bent on making her crash.

She felt the wheels skidding, saw the embankment coming up at her at a furious speed. She heard a scream and it only registered a beat later that the scream was coming from her.

The next moment Bailey hit her head on the dashboard and passed out.

The driver slowed and then came to a complete stop. He backed up his car so that he was parallel to the area where the other car had gone down the embankment.

He wanted to view firsthand the damage he had caused. From his vantage point, it didn't look as if the woman inside the mangled car was moving. Maybe she was dead.

"Good." He nodded and smiled to himself. "You had that coming, bitch. Just like that no-good, sanctimonious 'cowboy' of yours deserved everything he got when that overpriced whore was found on his property." His face clouded over. "Somebody ruined my plan with that stupid 'confession.' But don't worry—I'll find another way to take him out. Too bad you won't be alive to see it."

The area was still deserted.

He got out of his car, debating whether to go down the incline to make sure she was dead or if he shouldn't even bother and just set the car on fire.

One way or another, it would look like she'd lost control of her car and died. A fire would get rid of any evidence.

The best part, he thought, grinning with self-satisfaction, was that all this would be blamed on one of the people who had formed that mob in front of Colton's ranch house. Not everyone there had been placated when Cynthia had turned up. And not everyone had bought into that guy's written confession they'd found next to his body after he'd committed suicide.

He wasn't the one who'd killed her.

He had seen who'd killed Bianca, but there was no reason to rat the killer out. It didn't serve his purpose.

Yet.

Using the dead woman's body, though, would

have served a perfect purpose if things had gone according to plan.

This time he was going to have his way. Colton's ex-wife was going to die out here if she wasn't dead already. And then—

The sedan driver stopped, cocking his head and listening.

Damn it, someone was coming!

Torn between setting the car on fire or making good his escape, he knew he had to choose the latter. Otherwise he risked being caught, and if that happened, it would ruin all of his plans of revenge.

Cursing a blue streak, he hurried back to his sedan and quickly drove away.

He kept his eyes on the rearview mirror just in case the vehicle that was approaching was just another driver passing through on the way to somewhere else.

The next moment he realized that it wasn't just another driver. It was one of the sheriff's deputies.

Damn it all to hell!

He drove away quickly.

Deputy Jake Ross brought his car to a sudden stop.

He saw the skid marks. They went straight over the embankment. Jake got out and cautiously walked up to the edge of the incline.

The next moment he ran back to his car, calling for reinforcements on his radio.

* * *

Maybe it wasn't all bad, the man who'd forced Bailey's car off the road thought. Maybe that she devil was dead. At least, he could hope.

He couldn't hang around to find out.

"Yes, there's been an accident. I need help— and an ambulance. Bailey Norton, Wyatt's ex, was in some kind of an accident. Her car looks pretty banged up from here. I can see her inside, but it doesn't look like she's moving."

As he spoke, Jake looked up and down the road, but he didn't see anyone passing by. "We're going to need the fire department's help. Hurry! It's an emergency!" the deputy said. "I'm going to make my way down the incline, see if I can reach her. Get somebody here as fast as you can," he ordered.

Finished with the communication, the deputy walked to the edge of the incline again. He looked for a way to make it down to the unconscious woman in the totaled vehicle.

It wasn't going to be easy. The fact that there was still some snow left on the ground just complicated matters.

He really hoped the emergency vehicles got out here quickly.

Chapter 22

Wyatt felt really good.

For the first time in days he was no longer under the shadow of suspicion. The investigation revolving around the high-priced escort's murder was closed, and Trey had found Cynthia Gates, which had solved the second case against him before it had really gotten out of hand.

The cherry on the sundae was having Everett Olson arrested. Wyatt had just finished pressing charges against the rancher for the willful poisoning of his prize bull as well as going to great lengths in attempting to harm the rest of his herd.

As he started to leave Trey's office, Wyatt was smiling broadly. He couldn't wait to tell Bailey that it was all behind them and they could get back to "making that baby."

"Wyatt," Fox cried, bursting into the sheriff's office just as he was ready to leave. "You've got to come with me. It's Bailey."

And just like that, that good feeling Wyatt was experiencing vanished into thin air.

"What about Bailey?" His intuition told him that it wasn't going to be good.

Fox turned on his heel and was already leading the way outside to his vehicle. He looked at Wyatt over his shoulder. "There's been an accident."

A thousand different fragmented thoughts dashed in and out of his brain, each one worse than the one that came before it. Wyatt grabbed Fox's arm, turning the man around.

"What kind of an accident?" Wyatt demanded. There was a slight tremor in his voice.

"Deputy Ross said someone ran her off the road, Wyatt," Fox told him. "He was there, on the scene, just after it happened. It looks like she lost control of the vehicle and went over the embankment."

Wyatt's stomach dropped as the words registered. He felt numb.

"Is she…is she—?"

Wyatt couldn't get himself to ask the question because as long as it wasn't out there in the universe, there was still a chance that Bailey was alive.

He clung to that.

"Lucky for her, Jake came by just then. He called the emergency crew. They got there as fast as possible. Jake and the crew got her out of the car and to the hospital just in time." Fox searched his face to see if what he was saying was getting through to Wyatt. "It sounded like she got hurt, but thanks to the doctors there, it looks like she's going to come through it all just fine. If Deputy Ross hadn't come along when he had, her car would have crashed at the bottom of the embankment."

Trey had come out of his office, looking for Wyatt to find out why he had left so abruptly. What he had heard answered his question.

"I'll drive," he told Wyatt. In case the other man was going to demur, Trey said, "The siren and lights'll get us there faster."

Wyatt's brain was still in a fog, but he wasn't about to refuse the offer. He just wanted to get to the hospital. *Now* if not sooner.

"Bailey's a feisty little scrapper—we all know that. She's going to make it, Wyatt. You've got to believe that," Fox told him as he and Wyatt piled into Trey's police vehicle.

"Yeah."

There was no conviction in Wyatt's voice as he responded to Fox. But he had no choice. He *had* to hang on to what Fox had just said. The alternative was just too unbearable for him to contemplate.

The second Wyatt was inside the car, Trey gunned

the engine and they took off. But to Wyatt it felt as if the vehicle was being driven in slow motion. He felt as if he was about to jump out of his skin.

"Can't you make this damn thing go any faster?" he demanded.

"It's a car, Wyatt, not a plane. If I went any faster, this thing would take off the ground," Trey said. He glanced at his cousin and saw the anxious look on his face. "But I'll do my best."

Wyatt didn't trust himself to answer. He just nodded in response.

Feeling so tense that if he were a guitar string he would have snapped in two, Wyatt jumped out of the car the second Trey pulled up in front of the hospital.

Wyatt didn't wait for the others. Instead, he ran up to the automatic doors. They barely had time to open for him. Once inside, Wyatt went straight to the emergency admission desk.

"My wife was in a car accident," he told the woman behind the desk.

Trey and Fox exchanged glances, surprised that Wyatt was referring to Bailey as his wife rather than his ex-wife.

"She was just brought in," he was saying to the woman.

"Bailey Norton," Trey put in to facilitate the search.

The receptionist looked at the latest entries on the hospital log. Nodding, she told them, "Dr. Norton in trauma room two, Sheriff." She pointed to the hallway on her left.

Trey and Fox went with Wyatt down the hall but stopped just before the room the receptionist had specified.

"We'll wait out here for you," Trey said. "Take all the time you need."

"We'll be out here if you need us," Fox said, adding his voice to the sheriff's. "But you won't." He gave Wyatt a thumbs-up sign.

Wyatt stood facing the door and took a deep breath. The moment Fox had told him about the accident, he would have run all the way to get here. But now that he was right outside the room, he hesitated, afraid.

He gathered his courage together to face whatever he was about to find out.

He had no idea what was waiting for him on the other side of that door, but he was determined to be strong for Bailey no matter what.

Wyatt walked into the room, his heart in his throat. There was a doctor talking to Bailey.

The physician and Bailey both turned to look his way as he came in.

Bailey was crying. It was the first thing that he saw. His heart migrated into his chest and tightened. Whatever this was, he told himself, they were going to get through it.

Together.

"How is she, Doctor?" he asked the gray-haired man.

Rather than answer his question, Dr. Johnson glanced at Bailey. And then, in a voice that gave away nothing, he said, "I'll let her tell you." The next moment he slipped out, closing the door behind him.

There was a chair pushed to the side against the wall. Wyatt grabbed it, pulled it close to Bailey's bed and then sat.

"Oh, thank God. You scared the living daylights out of me!" he croaked. He took her hand in his, his eyes never leaving her face. "Are you all right?" Wyatt asked.

He kept his voice low, afraid that it would break if he spoke any louder. All his emotions felt as if they were perilously close to the surface.

To him it appeared that Bailey was attempting to muster a brave smile. *This is bad*, he thought.

"Yes."

"You're not just saying that because you know that's what I want to hear, are you?" he asked. "The doctor told you that you were all right, right?" Wyatt pressed.

"Well, he didn't exactly use those words," Bailey told him.

Wyatt braced himself. *Here it comes.*

"What did he say?" he asked. Before she could answer, he told her, "Because whatever it is, whatever he said, we'll face it together. I'm not going to let you go through this alone."

Confused, Bailey looked at him quizzically. "Then you know?"

They were talking at cross-purposes, he thought. "All I know is that I just had the fright of my life. I thought you were dead. But you're not. You're alive and breathing and that's *all* that matters to me. Whatever else it is, we'll handle it."

He took another breath, bracing himself. Whatever was wrong, no matter what, he wasn't about to let her panic or feel abandoned. He was going to be there with her every step of the way no matter what it took or how long it was.

"What did the doctor tell you?" he prompted, unable to put up with being in the dark any longer.

She had withdrawn her hand from his and now clasped her hands together as she answered his question. "He said that I'm pregnant."

Wyatt stared at her. To say that he was dumbfounded was an understatement. There had to be some kind of a miscommunication.

"Say again?"

"I'm pregnant," she repeated, this time with more emphasis.

He didn't understand. They had only made love that one time since she'd returned. Each time they were about to make love after that, they'd always been interrupted for one reason or another.

"But you said you had all those complicating factors interfering, that getting pregnant was going to be nothing short of a miracle," he reminded her. "Remember?"

She blinked back more tears. He wasn't freaking out or running out of the room. That was something, she thought. "I guess it's a miracle, then."

Stunned, he took her hands again. "Then it's true? You're really pregnant?"

The smile on her lips spread, widening as she repeated, "I'm really pregnant."

And then he remembered what she'd told him the day she had returned. She'd said that once she got pregnant, she was going to take off.

Bailey was going to leave, he realized, the thought hitting him with the force of a two-by-four being swung hard against his gut.

She saw the change in his expression immediately. Wyatt was regretting this, she thought. He was thinking of all the demands on him that would be made now that he'd fathered her child.

No, no jumping to conclusions, she upbraided herself. *Ask the man. Don't just assume his reaction.*

She struggled to gather her courage together. "What's the matter?" Bailey asked in a quiet voice.

He might as well say it, he thought. It was the elephant in the room.

"You'll be leaving now, won't you?" he said, his voice hollow, empty.

Bailey blinked, trying to comprehend what he'd just said. She hadn't been expecting him to say that.

Clearing her throat, she asked, "What?"

Why did she look like she didn't know what he was talking about? He was paraphrasing her own words. "Now that you've gotten what you came for, you'll be leaving. That's what you told me the first day you came back."

She remembered, but she'd been hoping he'd forgotten about that. Obviously not. Maybe that was the reason he'd slept with her in the first place, to get rid of her faster.

"Is that what you want?" she whispered.

"I want what you want and— No!" Wyatt said suddenly, his voice growing stronger. He was tired of saying what he thought she wanted him to say. She needed to hear *his* side of this. "I want you to stay. I want you to marry me all over again and be my wife, be the mother of my child. I want—"

Bailey's entire body ached like crazy, but she managed to pull herself up into a sitting position. She placed her fingers against his lips, stilling them.

He raised his eyebrows quizzically, looking at her.

"I want that, too," she told him.

"You do?" he asked, surprised, relieved.

"I do." Bailey placed her hand protectively against her very flat stomach. "We're a family now and I really want this. Don't worry—I'm not going to encroach on your space," she promised, anticipating his reaction. "I can open up my practice here while you run your ranch. We're both independent people but that doesn't mean we can't be together, as well." She smiled at him. "We've grown in those six years we spent apart. Grown as people, and we're both stronger for it.

"But I don't want to be a strong, independent person if it means being without you. Maybe I shouldn't say it, but I love you, Wyatt Colton, and I want our baby to love you. That can only happen if we stay together." Her eyes searched his face. "What do you think?"

"What do I think?" Wyatt repeated. "I'll tell you what I think." Unable to maintain a solemn facade any longer, he laughed. "I think it's a great plan."

He drew her very carefully into his arms so as not to hurt her. "Because I never stopped loving you even when I hated you for walking out on us. And I know, no matter what, that I'm going to go on loving you for the rest of my life." He framed her face with his hands. "It would make things a lot easier for me if you were here."

Bailey laughed, giddy with relief. The sound rumbled against his chest as she rested her cheek on it. "Lucky for you that fits in perfectly with my plan."

He raised her head again, putting the crook of his finger under her chin, until Bailey's eyes were level with his.

"Very lucky," he agreed. He lowered his mouth to hers and kissed her, sealing the bargain they had just struck. And gratefully sealing his fate with hers.

"So, how soon do you want the wedding?"

"Soon," she told him. "Very soon."

He smiled into her eyes, his heart so full it felt as if it was on the verge of bursting. "Can't be soon enough for me."

"Amen to that," she said softly just as he kissed her again.

This time the kiss had "forever" all over it, which was just fine with her.

* * * * *

Don't miss the next volume in the
Coltons of Roaring Springs series:

Colton Under Fire
by Cindy Dees.

Available from Harlequin Romantic Suspense
in February 2019!

COMING NEXT MONTH FROM

H HARLEQUIN®

ROMANTIC suspense

Available February 5, 2019

#2027 COLTON UNDER FIRE
The Coltons of Roaring Springs
by Cindy Dees
The signs all point to a serial killer loose in Roaring Springs, and Sloane Colton fits the victim profile much too closely. Detective Liam Kastor is determined to save her, but they'll have to learn to trust each other—and their flaring attraction— if they hope to escape the serial killer's crosshairs.

#2028 NAVY SEAL TO THE RESCUE
Aegis Security • by Tawny Weber
Headhunter Lila Adrian's career is on a roll, until she witnesses the murder of her latest target! Former SEAL Travis Hawkins is the only person who believes she's in danger, and together, they have to find the murderer and get out of Costa Rica alive—no matter what it takes.

#2029 GUARDING HIS WITNESS
Bachelor Bodyguards • by Lisa Childs
Rosie Mendez won't live to testify against her brother's killer unless she allows bodyguard Clint Quarters to protect her, but she holds him as responsible for her brother's death as the man who actually pulled the trigger. Can she allow him close to her long enough to make it to the witness stand alive?

#2030 SHIELDED BY THE LAWMAN
True Blue • by Dana Nussio
Having escaped from the abusive ex-husband whom the police protected, Sarah Cline and her young son, Aiden, find an unlikely safe place with an atoning rookie cop, who helps to shield them from a bigger threat than she ever realized.

YOU CAN FIND MORE INFORMATION ON UPCOMING HARLEQUIN® TITLES, **FREE EXCERPTS AND MORE AT WWW.HARLEQUIN.COM.**

HRSCNM0119

Get 4 FREE REWARDS!

We'll send you 2 FREE Books
plus 2 FREE Mystery Gifts.

Harlequin® Romantic Suspense books feature heart-racing sensuality and the promise of a sweeping romance set against the backdrop of suspense.

FREE
Value Over
$20

YES! Please send me 2 FREE Harlequin® Romantic Suspense novels and my 2 FREE gifts (gifts are worth about $10 retail). After receiving them, if I don't wish to receive any more books, I can return the shipping statement marked "cancel." If I don't cancel, I will receive 4 brand-new novels every month and be billed just $4.99 per book in the U.S. or $5.74 per book in Canada. That's a savings of at least 12% off the cover price! It's quite a bargain! Shipping and handling is just 50¢ per book in the U.S. and 75¢ per book in Canada.* I understand that accepting the 2 free books and gifts places me under no obligation to buy anything. I can always return a shipment and cancel at any time. The free books and gifts are mine to keep no matter what I decide.

240/340 HDN GMYZ

Name (please print)

Address   Apt. #

City   State/Province   Zip/Postal Code

Mail to the Reader Service:
IN U.S.A.: P.O. Box 1341, Buffalo, NY 14240-8531
IN CANADA: P.O. Box 603, Fort Erie, Ontario L2A 5X3

Want to try 2 free books from another series! Call 1-800-873-8635 or visit www.ReaderService.com.

*Terms and prices subject to change without notice. Prices do not include sales taxes, which will be charged (if applicable) based on your state or country of residence. Canadian residents will be charged applicable taxes. Offer not valid in Quebec. This offer is limited to one order per household. Books received may not be as shown. Not valid for current subscribers to Harlequin® Romantic Suspense books. All orders subject to approval. Credit or debit balances in a customer's account(s) may be offset by any other outstanding balance owed by or to the customer. Please allow 4 to 6 weeks for delivery. Offer available while quantities last.

Your Privacy—The Reader Service is committed to protecting your privacy. Our Privacy Policy is available online at www.ReaderService.com or upon request from the Reader Service. We make a portion of our mailing list available to reputable third parties that offer products we believe may interest you. If you prefer that we not exchange your name with third parties, or if you wish to clarify or modify your communication preferences, please visit us at www.ReaderService.com/consumerschoice or write to us at Reader Service Preference Service, P.O. Box 9062, Buffalo, NY 14240-9062. Include your complete name and address.

HRS19R

SPECIAL EXCERPT FROM

ⒽHARLEQUIN®

ROMANTIC suspense

Headhunter Lila Adrian's career is on a roll, until she witnesses the murder of her latest target! Former SEAL Travis Hawkins is the only person who believes she's in danger, and together, they have to find the murderer and get out of Costa Rica alive—no matter what it takes.

Read on for a sneak preview of
New York Times *bestselling author Tawny Weber's first book in her new Aegis Security series,*
Navy SEAL to the Rescue.

"I think I might be pretty good at motivating myself," Lila confessed.

"Everybody should know how to motivate themselves," Travis agreed with a wicked smile. "Aren't you going to ask about my stress levels?"

"Are you stressed?" she asked, taking one step backward.

"That depends."

"Depends on what?"

"On if you're interested in doing something about it." His smile sexy enough to make her light-headed, he moved forward one step.

Since his legs were longer than hers, his step brought him close enough to touch. To feel. To taste.

She held her breath when he reached out. He shifted his gaze to his fingers as they combed through her hair, swirling one long strand around and around. His gaze met hers again and he gave a tug.

"So?" he asked quietly. "Interested?"

"I shouldn't be. This would probably be a mistake," she murmured, her eyes locked on his mouth. His lips looked so soft, a contrast against those dark whiskers. Were they soft, too? How would they feel against her skin?

Desire wrapped around her like a silk ribbon, pretty and tight.

"Let's see what it feels like making a mistake together." With that, his mouth took hers.

The kiss was whisper soft. The lightest teasing touch of his lips to hers. Pressing, sliding, enticing. Then his tongue slid along her bottom lip in a way that made Lila want to purr. She straight up melted, the trembling in her knees spreading through her entire body.

Don't miss
Navy SEAL to the Rescue *by Tawny Weber,*
available February 2019 wherever
Harlequin® Romantic Suspense books
and ebooks are sold.

www.Harlequin.com

Copyright © 2019 by Tawny Weber

HRSEXP0119

HARLEQUIN®

ROMANTIC suspense
Heart-racing romance, breathless suspense

Don't miss this riveting True Blue story by Dana Nussio

One conflicted cop must protect a woman living a lie

Trooper Jamie Donovan suspects there's more to Sarah Cline than the waitress reveals. And Sarah, on the run with her son from an abusive ex-husband, won't trust Jamie with the truth. But when danger– greater than she realized—catches up to Sarah, Jamie confronts the biggest dilemma of his life: uphold his oath or aid and abet the woman he loves?

Available February 2019

www.Harlequin.com

HRSBPA0119

Need an adrenaline rush from nail-biting tales
(and irresistible males)?

Check out **Harlequin Intrigue®**,
Harlequin® Romantic Suspense and
Love Inspired® Suspense books!

New books available every month!

CONNECT WITH US AT:

Facebook.com/groups/HarlequinConnection

 Facebook.com/HarlequinBooks

 Twitter.com/HarlequinBooks

 Instagram.com/HarlequinBooks

 Pinterest.com/HarlequinBooks

ReaderService.com

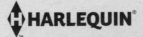

**ROMANCE WHEN
YOU NEED IT**

SGENRE2018R